I0677418

SINCERELY CLAIRE

Jean Ann Williams

Love Truth

Copyright © 2020: Jean Ann Williams

ISBN: 978-0-9977016-5-4

Cover Illustration by Danniel Campbell
Cover Designed by Louis Edwards
Edited by Barbara Oden & Edie Sodowsky
Format by Lee Carver

Scripture quotations from The Authorized (King James) Version. Rights in the Authorized Version in the United Kingdom are vested in the Crown. Reproduced by permission of the Crown's patentee, Cambridge University Press

This is a work of fiction. Names, places, characters, and events are fictitious in every regard. Any similarities to actual events and persons, living or dead, are purely coincidental. Any trademarks, service marks, product names, or named features are assumed to be the property of their respective owners, and are used only for reference. There is no implied endorsement if any of these terms are used. Except for review purposes, the reproduction of this book in whole or part, electronically or mechanically, constitutes a copyright violation.

I dedicate this sequel of Just Claire *to my son, Joshua Williams, who has gone on to the Great Beyond. I miss him more than words can express. November 27, 1978 — March 16, 2004.*

Acknowledgements

To my wonderful and smart daughter Jami who suggested I begin the craft of writing in 1994. I'm especially grateful to my husband Jim, who has supported me emotionally in the highs and lows of writing and editing stories.

Finally, and above all, thank You, Lord, for caring about the little things which happen in life on Earth. You are my Rock.

SINCERELY CLAIRE
1961, Redwood Highway, Oregon

"We don't want a tardy slip on our first day." Claire opened the locker door and placed her sack lunch inside. Her friend, Lizbeth, nodded from two lockers over and then started to chat about her summer. With a sudden shove, Claire's locker door banged against her head. She stumbled but caught herself before she hit the ground. The hall spun.

"Oops." A hazy form appeared from around the half-closed door. "Well, if it isn't the grade flunker."

What? Not *that* voice. Her head smarted and she blinked as her eyes adjusted. Oh. No. She let out a breath she'd been holding. Please, not her. Shoulders rigid, shock and denial coursed through her like a winding stream. Her mouth dropped open. Could she do this again? She had hoped that leaving Gallagher Springs, California, behind had meant leaving the girl with the mean, hateful voice behind as well. She touched her head and winced. "Shouldn't you be home in Boston? Didn't your dad finish his job when mine did?"

"Well, ClaireLee, what kind of greeting is that?"

Lizbeth leaned near Claire's ear while steadying her wobbly feet. "That had to have hurt." She whispered, "How does she know you?"

She bowed her head near Lizbeth's ear. "It's a long story, but I can tell you she's a bully."

Lizbeth gasped, "Surely not."

The mean girl's toe nudged Claire's shoe. "I sure didn't intend to hit your head. I sort of stumbled against your locker door." She smirked, right when Lizbeth turned her head away.

She's still a bully and a sneak.

A blonde, curly-mopped girl appeared beside the Toe Nudger. "Hi, ClaireLee. Fancy meeting you here."

Double oh, no.

The bell rang.

The few kids that stood nearby left, including the two girls who called her ClaireLee.

Lizbeth's soft voice came with her extended elbow. "Let's get to class. You can tell me during our lunch hour how those girls know you."

As they walked into the room, the two friends found desks where they could sit together.

The teacher clapped her hands. "Okay. Class, let's go around and introduce ourselves. I'm your homeroom teacher, Mrs. Byers. Do not call me by my first name, even though many of you know me. I'm not June to you. Never. I'm Mrs. Byers, to show respect." She aimed her chin toward her black low-heeled shoes. She glanced around the room, her thin lips turned down. "Even when we meet out of this school environment, you are to call me Mrs. Byers. Is that understood?"

A chorus of voices rang out. "Yes, Mrs. Byers."

As Claire lowered her aching forehead into her cupped hands, a loud snicker came from behind. She could guess who that was. Bully Kaye Tyner. Did she really not mean to shove into her locker door and hit her in the head?

Dear Lord, have mercy. And Kaye wasn't alone either. She came with her friend, Wendy Lavender.

Mrs. Byers nodded. "I see at least two new faces to our community. Stand for us and tell your name and a bit about yourself."

Wendy stood with the grace of a queen, then sniffed. "My name is Wendy Lavender. Like the flower lavender." She raised her nose a bit higher. "My father is one of the bosses for the current tunnel being built near the Oregon state line." She touched the collar of her blue, velvet dress. "I'm from the city of Boston." She looked down her nose at a few of the students. "And in case you aren't aware, Boston is an important cultural and historical city in Massachusetts." She patted the curls around her face and sat back down in her seat.

It seemed like Mrs. Byers smiled her approval. Claire had to keep from rolling her eyes. Good grief. If the teacher only knew Wendy, she'd turn several shades of purple.

"You, young lady, with the corded jumper are next."

She stood. "I'm Kaye Tyner." She opened a palm and aimed it at Wendy. "Wendy is my best friend. I also live in Boston. She and I grew up together, and our dads are the bosses for the tunnel crew." She pursed her lips. "We've had the privilege of attending the best private school in the most outstanding city in the United States." She rotated her head—ever so slight—and sat down. Then popped back up like a deranged jack-in-the-box. "And I just want to say I can't wait to meet everyone personally."

Mrs. Byers' smile grew.

Claire couldn't resist an eye roll. If Mrs. Byers knew about Kaye, she'd probably faint. Brother. This school was not ready for those two.

After everyone stood and introduced themselves, Mrs. Byers asked Kaye to pass out papers for the homeroom rules.

She hurried to the teacher's desk and grabbed the stack. She went to each desk and handed the students their papers. At a desk near Claire, Kaye said, "Nice dress, Holly." She continued around the room. Once again, she spoke. "Hi Lizbeth. I really like your green hair ribbon." It got quiet for a second, so Claire turned in her seat. Kaye whispered near Lizbeth's ear, and they both chuckled.

Her chest steamed with anger. She would have a hard time explaining to Lizbeth what a bully Kaye was if she acted nice.

Before Kaye handed Claire her papers, she bent close and whispered, "I'm going to steal Lizbeth from you, ClaireLee." She spread her mouth into a fake smile.

She gritted her teeth so hard they crunched and at the same time grabbed the papers from Kaye's hand. It was not easy to make her face a mask of indifference.

Would this be a repeat of school last year in Gallagher Springs?

~∧~∧~

Claire joined Lizbeth on the lunch bench as they sat side by side. "I thought this morning would never end." Lizbeth opened her colorful lunch pail. Claire dug into her less-festive brown paper bag. Her mouth watered at the donut treat she placed on her napkin. Her family had more money since Daddy got a job building the new tunnel twenty miles into Northern California from the Oregon border. The best part was he could drive to and from work each day. No moving to a new place like with his last tunnel job.

Lizbeth broke into her thoughts. "So. I know now how Kaye and Wendy know you."

She met Lizbeth's gaze and waited for her to continue.

"Are you ready to tell me why you keep saying they are bullies?"

She twisted in her seat and scanned the cafeteria. She had to make sure the bullies were nowhere in sight. The two rich girls probably went across the road to get lunch at the drugstore's cafe. "I still have to say it's a long story."

She stalled to gather her thoughts and to take a bite of her tuna sandwich made with Mama's whole wheat bread. After she chewed and swallowed, she began. "Those two girls? They are not nice. Especially Kaye who lied about accidently banging the locker door against my head."

Claire laid down her sandwich. "Wendy Lavender likes power. She'll get it anyway she can—like acting nice to get her way. And that Kaye Tyner? She's a follower who likes being around power, but she has a hateful side which is much worse than Wendy's." She picked at the bread crust. "Sometimes I wonder if Wendy would be nicer if she wasn't around Kaye."

Lizbeth frowned and removed the wax paper from her sandwich, but set it down again. "But Kaye seems really nice, so I'm confused."

Claire stiffened, remembering what Kaye said about stealing Lizbeth's friendship from her. She needed to relax. Breathe. Close her eyes for a few seconds. "I know. Why don't you ask me questions? Things you want to know about them. Might be easier."

"Okay." She took a quick bite, chewed, and swallowed. "So they were in the same town as you because of the tunnel being built?"

"Yes." She blinked. "Uh-oh."

Lizbeth leaned so their shoulders touched. "What?" When she didn't answer right away, she pressed her arm against hers. "Tell me."

"It can't be. It just can't be so. I just realized those two girls *will* be here the whole school year." She placed her hands around the ache in her head. "Daddy told me this job won't be finished until the middle of next summer."

Lizbeth scrunched her brows. "But I still don't think they're so bad."

She crossed her arms on the table, nestled her forehead there, and moaned. "I understand that's what you see right now." She moved to place her cheek on her arms and face Lizbeth. "I thought I had gotten rid of them. I thought what a wonderful time I'd have this school year. I was so happy when last school year was over." She jerked upright. The pain caused her to suck air through her teeth. "I can't do this."

Lizbeth touched her hand. "Even though I wasn't there to see what they did to you, I will stand by you no matter what."

"Thank you." She considered the rest of her lunch, and her stomach churned with nausea. "I'm not hungry." She wrapped her half-eaten sandwich and stuffed it back into her brown paper bag. "I'm doomed. They're even in my homeroom class."

"We're in that class together though. It'll be okay. Your sandwich looked yummy. Wish my mom would make homemade bread more often."

"It's not that. It was tasty, but talking about Gallagher Springs and seeing those girls have followed me back home … I-I feel sick."

"I don't think they had a choice, do you?" Lizbeth extended her open hand. "Especially with their dads working near here and all."

"Maybe. Maybe not. They told me they chose to come with their dads on the last tunnel job." She nibbled on her fingernail. "I'm shocked, really, that they would go another school year without their precious highfalutin schools and shopping galore." Although, this made her wonder if the girls had been honest with her back in Gallagher Springs about why they were with their dads.

Lizbeth finished her lunch and wiped her mouth with a napkin. "I can't imagine such unkind girls. And though you haven't told me the whole story, your reactions make me think things were horrid." She tapped the table. "But still, I can't judge them unless I see this bullying for myself."

Claire blew at her bangs as it became hot in the room. "That's fair."

The two friends stood and picked up their lunch pail and brown paper bag. She motioned for Lizbeth to lead the way. "It would take hours for me to tell you all that happened."

And some of it was about my mother.

"Why don't we keep to ourselves? Stay as far away from those two as possible." They kept walking, and she looked around again to see if the mean girls were nearby. "I give you my word, they will come after me. And when they come after me, they will come after you." Goosebumps raised along her skin. "Lizbeth, if Kaye is able, she'll tear our friendship to shreds."

2

"Surely not." Lizbeth pushed open the cafeteria doors. "Those girls don't even know me." As they stepped onto the covered walkway, Lizbeth hooked arms with Claire. A crowd of boys playing basketball on the outdoor court erupted with shouts and yays. Lizbeth continued, "Besides, I go where you go. You are my best friend, and I missed you while you were gone."

"Thank you, Lizbeth." She inhaled a sharp breath. "And I'm sorry about telling you bad stuff about them. But that's how they operate. I'm afraid they're going to try to take you away from me and become the most popular girls in seventh grade."

She shook her head. "I don't believe you." She walked on as Claire kept in step. "At least I don't want to believe you."

Claire nudged her to stop. "We really need Belinda here. With the three of us, we could be a three-cord-strength against their pranks."

Lizbeth steered her around the school building to a quiet spot away from the basketball court and kickball pad area. "I remember you writing to me about Belinda." She leaned against school the wall. "She was a good friend to you back in Gallagher Springs. Right?"

"Yes. And her grandmother is one of the nicest ladies ever." She snapped her fingers. "I have the perfect—"

The bell rang for the students to get back to their classes.

She bent close to her ear. "When I get home, I'm writing Belinda a letter."

~∿∧∿~

"I've been learnin' how to doctor Bossy's leg so we won't have to put her down."

Claire lay crossways on the bed and pressed Belinda's long-awaited letter to her chest. *Poor, poor Bossy. They can't lose such a good milk cow.* She raised the letter to finish reading out loud.

"Bossy fell down a gully and banged her leg but good. Even has a deep gash on her knee."

Right at that moment, her little sister, Lolly, came into her bedroom—Laddie, their German shepherd, trotted behind. "Who's Bossy, Sissy Pie?"

She sat upright. "Please leave. It's not nice to eavesdrop on a person's private letters." Laddie rushed to her and sniffed, wagging his tail.

But her sister's bottom lip poked out as she crossed her arms over her chest. Tears glistened within her lashes. "I, I sorry, Sissy Pie."

She jumped off the bed and grabbed her in a hug. "Okay, okay." She kneeled to her little sister's level. "Now you do know, huh?"

Her head bobbed up and down against Claire's chest.

Laddie shoved his muzzle between them, and she opened her arms for a group hug. "Sometimes people need private time, honey."

She glanced up. Her tears broke loose, rolled along her cheeks, and disappeared to the hardwood floor. Claire bowed her head in shame for being so gruff. Two tiny puddles shimmered inches from Lolly's bare and dirty toes.

Laddie licked the moisture off the floor.

"I will let you read. In private." She twisted to break away from Claire, grabbed Laddie's collar, and shut the door behind them.

Whew. That ended well.

For a while, she gazed at the peeling paint on the back of the closed door. She knew the move back home from Gallagher Springs was good. But reading Belinda's letter made her homesick for her newest friend.

She sighed. It was time to read more news she'd been waiting on for over a month. And then she would write her back to share the idea sticking to her brain like a wad of chewing gum on the underside of a school desk.

She laid on her back on the bed, being careful not to muss the quilt she and Mama had made. She read Belinda's words. In silence.

Oh, Claire. I can't wait for school to start next week. It's lonely out here with just me and Grandma Neecy. There is no one like you for a buddy. The only best part of this

*school year is all the other tunnel workers' kids are gone.
Not only will there be fewer kids, but no more Lavender
Girls.*

Claire stared at her knotty pine ceiling. If she only
knew where those girls had landed.

Wendy and Kaye had taken over the tiny school and
bullied anyone not under their rule. And they were good at
stealing friends—they almost stole her from Belinda. But
Claire understood what they were doing before it was too
late.

She imagined Belinda's big, toothy grin. With her
last thoughts about where the Lavender Girls were this year,
she could envision her friend's puckered expression. Oh,
how her heart ached to see her buddy again.

She needed Belinda to help at home and at school.

Claire squeezed her eyes shut and imagined the three
of them together. Her, Lizbeth, and Belinda. The thought
bolted her upright. They could start their own club at school.
They could outsmart those Lavender Girls. She tapped her
chin. What should they call themselves?

No way would she use one of their last names like
Wendy Lavender had done. That was too much like a
copycat. She'd have to run her club idea by Lizbeth.

Another thought struck. She believed Belinda would
like seventh grade in Kerbyville. Where the Monteiro's lived
in Selmac, ten miles south of Kerbyville, it was a bit bigger
than Gallagher Springs. They had a market, which also held
a post office and a café. The best part? Belinda would love
living on the property with ninety-nine acres to roam.

After reading Belinda's letter, she sat at her tiny desk across from the foot of her bed. She pulled lined school paper and her pencil from the drawer. She wrote back to her good friend what sounded like a dream.

Dreams could come true. Right?

September 10

Dear Belinda, we should talk your grandma into you two living with us this school year. You and Grandma Neecy could help me with running our house. We'd be together and have fun too.

Mama still gets under the weather because of her bouts with sadness. So I have to run things when she's in her room sleeping. Thank goodness it's only happened twice since we left Gallagher Springs. Course, we've only been gone since June.

I like my school. It is two grades—seventh and eighth, so we have a whole building to ourselves.

But I do have bad news. You will not believe who has moved to Oregon. I hope you are not eating while you read this because you will spit your food all over this letter and won't be able to finish reading it. You might even fall over dead when you read this. Poor Grandma Neecy will have to breathe air into your mouth to wake you.

Kaye Tyner and Wendy Lavender live here!!! They did not go home to Boston.

I need you here for more than to help me with Mama. With me, you, and my friend, Lizbeth (who will like you, and you both will become best friends), we could set those Lavender Girls straight. Once and for all and forever.

Claire lifted her hand and twiddled her pencil between her fingers. What else could she write about? What else was as important as asking Belinda and her grandma to come live with them? Nothing. But. The letter was too short. She bent her head over the paper.

I will talk to Daddy and see if you can live with us. So, I will not finish this letter until I get an answer from him.

~∧~∧~∧

The next day as Claire rode her bus to junior high, she worried. She wasn't able to finish her letter to Belinda. Daddy worked late, again, and his new job was like last time. He used dynamite to blast through the mountain and make a tunnel in the middle of another wilderness. It would make the route to the California Coast much faster because it would be less of a winding road.

A bigger concern for the day would be to handle the Lavender Girls.

Would they leave her alone? If not, would Lizbeth be any kind of match against them? Would she have to protect Lizbeth from Kaye and Wendy? And why did she keep thinking of them as the Lavender Girls Club? There was only the two of them. Not the former three like they were in Gallagher Springs.

They were in her territory now.

Still, she needed Belinda. Even though Claire was stronger, but shorter, than Lizbeth, Belinda was the tallest and strongest girl ever. They could become like the Three Musketeers, fighting for justice in a cruel world.

When she got off the bus, someone behind her yelled, "Boo."

Claire jumped and would have surely swallowed her tongue if it hadn't been attached. She twirled to face Lizbeth and let her grin stretch as wide as the Illinois River near Selmac.

She pressed a hand to her throat. "You scared the life out of me." She hugged her old friend good morning, and she returned the hug with a squeeze.

"Well? Did you write the letter to Belinda? What did you write about?"

She grabbed Lizbeth's hand and hurried them along. "We have to make a plan."

"A plan?" Lizbeth kept pace with her. "For what?" They climbed the wide steps which lead into the building with the other students.

Once inside, they huddled in a quiet corner by the secretary's office. "Listen, Lizbeth, we can't just think Kaye and Wendy will leave us alone. They won't. They hate me."

Lizbeth nibbled on her bottom lip. "Why do they feel that way?"

She glanced at the large clock on the wall. "We have only five minutes until the bell rings. I don't have time to explain." She felt the bump on the side of her head from yesterday. "It still smarts. But never mind. This is what we have to do above all else." She gripped her friend's arms and stared into her hazel eyes. "We stay together."

"You said that yesterday." She blinked. "We would anyway."

"Yes. Even if we have to use the bathroom, we go together. The Lavender Girls pull their worst tricks in the bathroom away from anyone else noticing."

"Not a problem." She shrugged. "What else?"

"If you ever get caught alone with them, don't speak. Don't say a word. Pretend you are deaf. Keep walking. Got it?"

Her lashes fluttered. "You're making me nervous."

"I'm sorry." She touched her friend's shoulder. "I have too much experience with them. And just so you know, and to make matters worse, one night I humiliated Kaye in front of the whole school."

"What?" She drew back from her. "What did she do to deserve that?"

Staring at her shoes, she folded her arms across her waist. "She embarrassed Mama. In front of the whole school."

Lizbeth covered her gasp with her hand, and her eyes grew moist. "That's the cruelest thing I've ever heard. Your mama is a saint."

"Thank you for saying so." She allowed a moment of silence, in deep respect for her wonderful mama. "This is how mean Kaye can be, so stick by me and maybe you'll be okay."

That is, Claire could only hope and pray.

3

She nibbled on her ragged fingernail and studied the clock again. The bell rang ten minutes after eight to start a new school day.

She squeezed Lizbeth's hand. "Let's wait until most of the kids are at their desks. That way Kaye and Wendy will be ahead and not behind us." She leaned against the wall near the classroom door, and her friend followed her example. "At least we're in the same first class like you said."

After the boy who slept through class straggled in, she gave Lizbeth the thumbs up sign. As they rounded the opened door, Kaye stepped in front of them. She frowned and opened her mouth wide as though ready to cut them to shreds with her tongue.

Mrs. Byers waved them in. "Hurry inside, girls."

As Claire entered the room, she scanned the faces and found Wendy waggling her fingers at her without a hint of a smile. And when Kaye sat down next to her, they both stared at her and smirked.

Lord, you've got to help me be nice.

Mrs. Byers gave her morning speech about how there was to be no talking in class and all eyes were to watch her when she spoke. And especially no sleeping. She glared at the boy who broke that rule. As the teacher droned on about other rules, Claire's mind roamed.

She could hardly wait to find out why Wendy and Kaye were here instead of home in Boston. Did their moms decide to live with them? Last year, their moms stayed behind while the two girls went to Gallagher Springs with their dads.

She sighed. Because of them, she would spend the entire year on the defense. Unless. Unless somehow she stopped them early on. Make it clear they would not rule this class like they did at Belinda's school in Gallagher Springs.

She straightened her shoulders. Claire would not go through seventh grade like she did sixth grade. She'd been such a silly and almost lost Belinda's friendship.

Mrs. Byers was saying something interesting. . . . "and some of you are also in my English class."

Claire sat higher in her seat. English?

The teacher walked over to a large stack of shiny books. A new book would perk her up any ol' day.

"Mr. Swanson."

"Yeah?" The sleepy boy lifted his gaze.

"Please pass out these books. And it's not yeah, but yes, ma'am." She glared at him. "In my classes we use proper grammar. I detest slang. And I better never, ever hear you say the a-i-n-'t word."

As Mrs. Byers continued on about other words she would not tolerate, Claire's thoughts wandered again. Maybe it won't be like last year. Maybe Kaye learned her lesson about being a bully. Then, again, maybe not. Hadn't she made herself known by banging the locker door into her head? She puckered her mouth. She wanted to spit at the thought of such mean gestures.

If only Belinda were here to help her against the meanest bullies she had ever known.

~^~^~

That afternoon after school, Claire finished her letter to Belinda. She signed it and added a P.S.

Please tell your grandma that Daddy liked her help last time so he will this time. Mama still gets overwhelmed with the kids, a baby, and a big house to run. Daddy has been working on part of his shop to turn into an apartment so you and your grandma will have your own place. Please write me soon and let me know if you can come live with us.

She dug through her vanity table drawer and separated one stamp from the three she had left. She licked the glue side and pressed it on the right corner of the envelope. Because the glue on the envelope tasted yucky, she shuddered. She pressed the seal with the side of her palm and let out a soft breath. The letter to Belinda was done. Sandals nearby, she slipped her feet into them and slid the letter into her skirt pocket.

Claire headed outside and walked the long driveway to their mailbox. The apples in their orchard were still green with a few yellow and reds. She could smell them ripening, and her mouth watered.

A whistle tweet sounded near Clear Creek's bridge. But no one was in the water near there in the swimming hole, and a movement drew her vision elsewhere. Her brothers and Laddie ran toward her direction.

Liam hollered, "Over here, Claire." Laddie yipped at her and licked her arm.

Within twenty feet of the boys, she strained to see anything that could have excited them. Liam bent and grabbed a stick. He twirled it around as both boys laughed. The "stick" curled upward and moved like a rope in slow motion as he passed it to their little brother.

She halted right there and took a backward step. "Ah, no. You know I hate those slippery, stinky things."

Grayson stared at it in his hand. "Oh Claire, this kind of snake doesn't stink."

She pinched her nose between her thumb and forefinger. "Yes, it does. All snakes stink." She dance-hopped a step from them. "Keep it away from—"

But now Liam had it and he whipped it at her. She screamed and covered her head with her arms. He laughed while her other brother giggled like a girl.

"Not funny." She hurried to the mailbox across the road, placed the letter inside, and raised the flag. She took a step and bumped into Liam—the snake in his hand curled to meet her face. Its head was so near as its tongue flicked. She screeched and jumped. "Boys. All they think about is reptiles and getting into trouble."

She moved past Liam and ran home.

∧∼∧∼∧

By Friday, Claire was ready for the first week of school to end. At the last bell, she and Lizbeth hurried to their lockers. Soon, she would board the bus for the twenty minute ride to her house in Selmac while Lizbeth took a ten minute bus ride to Cavern Junction.

Claire missed the summer freedoms of exploring their ninety-nine acres, with the land's deer trails, meadows, and a creek.

Junior high did not hold the same excitement as before—before the Lavender Girls crowded into Claire's territory.

∧∽∧∽∧

"But, Mama, Daddy taught me to milk the goat." The next morning, Claire and Laddie followed Mama to the miniature pole barn Daddy and the boys had built the weekend before. They wrapped the barn in high, sturdy fencing to keep in the goat, and they built a gate.

As they walked over a makeshift planked bridge across their dry stream bed, Mama cradled an empty quart jar in her arms. "Now Claire, I told your daddy I'd learn how to milk. And by golly, I will."

She was glad Mama seemed rested and happy today. But still….

She stepped onto solid ground on the other side of the bridge and faced Claire. "Your daddy laughed at me. Said I didn't know how to milk. That there was no reason for me to do outside chores because you would do the milking." Her mouth twitched. "I'll show him I can handle a goat."

Claire touched the quart jar. "Let me carry it for you, Mama."

"I'm not a weakling." She shrugged off her hand and continued to walk. "I can carry an empty jar for heaven's sake."

Claire pursed her mouth and kept in step with her. "How about I start the milking so you can see how it's done? Then you can take over?"

Silence. Okay. Maybe not. "What's the goat's name? Daddy did say you could name her."

She stopped and pressed a hand to her side. "Oh, I've got a stitch from walking too fast." She bent forward and heaved a breath. "What did you ask?"

"If the goat had a name." She lifted the jar from her mother's arms.

"Goat." She approached the goat barn.

"Are you teasing?" Claire took off after her.

"No," she chuckled. "She's called Goat."

At that moment, Goat bleated. When they reached the barn, Goat cried louder. Mama dug in her pocket and lifted out a carrot. "Here." Goat snapped the carrot in half with her teeth.

Claire leaned closer to Goat and peered inside her mouth. "Would you look at this. Something's wrong with Goat. She has no teeth on the top front."

"Really?" Mama angled her head. "Well, I'll be. Maybe this is the way with all goats. We'll have to ask your daddy. It's odd to not have top teeth."

She dug into her pocket again and pulled out a wet cloth wrapped in waxed paper. She washed her hands with the cloth and Goat's teats and pocketed the rag. "I need a stool. Would you get me one of the sawed-off logs next to the barn?"

After she hurried to reach the log pile, she rolled one to where Mama waited. "Thank you, Claire." She handed her two pieces of carrot. "Give Goat one and wait a bit until she fidgets and then give her the other. This will keep her happy while I milk." With a nod, she took the carrots.

Mama had tied Goat to the pole barn fence, then moved the log closer and settled onto it. She set the milk jar under Goat. "Here I go." She hunched closer to Goat and began an up-and-squeeze milking with three fingers.

Claire gasped. "How'd you know not to milk a goat like a cow?"

As the milk pinged in the bottom of the glass jar, Mama never took her eyes off her job. "I checked with our neighbor, Norma. It's an up on the teat and squeeze, not pull down as you do for cows."

Laddie sniffed near Goat's teat, and Mama elbowed him out of the way.

Claire made sure to space out the carrot treats for Goat. Mama had gotten a half quart of milk before Goat ate the last one. A good minute went by when Goat kicked a hind leg at the jar. It cracked. Another kick and Mama flew backwards and landed on a large rock.

Claire gasped and hurried to help her up. She adjusted her body from its awkward position and pulled the rock from underneath her. Her breaths were cut short as though she were in terrible pain. "Breathe, Mama, breathe."

Laddie whined and sniffed at the commotion. Claire pushed him. "Move, boy."

Time slowed. "I'm lifting your head." Mama swallowed and heaved in air. She groaned. Claire sat on the ground, lifted Mama's head, and eased it onto her lap.

Mama winced. "Ow."

She tried to soothe her and patted her shoulder. "Be still. You rest until you think you can stand." She bit her lower lip. Mama seemed more than a little hurt.

A breeze stirred the air and feathered her mother's silken black hair over her high cheek bones. Claire reached out a hand and brushed the strands from her pale face.

Goat bleated. Her udder still had milk, and her belly was most likely empty of food.

"This is your fault, so don't cry to me."

Mama attempted to sit. "I think," she gasped and cried out. "It's my hip."

"You're in too much pain for me to help you stand." Her heart pumped faster. "What should I do?"

Tears slid along the sides of her hairline. "Call Norma."

She eased out from under her head. "I'll tell Liam to bring you a blanket and pillow." She hoped those words would soothe Mama until she returned. "Stay here, Laddie boy."

The dog sat. Claire bolted and yelled for her brothers.

She found Liam in one of the apple trees with Grayson.

"What do you want?" Liam dug his teeth into another bite of a greenish yellow apple.

"Hurry. It's Mama." She stopped under the tree. "The goat kicked while Mama was milking, and she fell. It's her hip. Get a blanket and pillow for her and make her comfortable while I call Norma to come help."

Before she even finished talking, her brothers scrambled down the tree and sprinted. She ran to the house to call Norma.

~^~^~

"Your mama's hurt?" Norma's voice squeaked.

Much relieved Norma was home to answer the phone call, Claire let go of a sob. "Yes, please. Will you come over and help us?"

"Be right there." And the line disconnected with a click.

Claire settled the phone's handhold into its cradle. Should she run back to the pole barn? No. She hadn't told Norma where Mama lay injured. She wouldn't know where to look for them behind the house. It was only a two minute drive ... Norma would be here any moment.

At least so she prayed.

4

Claire rushed outside to the front steps. She tapped her bare toes and craned her neck to get the first glimpse of Norma's car. Before she spied it, the sound of the car puttered and sputtered.

Even at a time like this, she thought what she always had when she caught a glimpse of Norma's vehicle. The strangest vehile ever built. So much so that she'd asked her once what kind of car she drove. Norma puffed out her tiny chest and told her it was a 1956 Renault Dauphine. Now, as she kept track of its movement, it jerked as it sped from Redwood Highway onto the Monteiro driveway. The Renault slid to a stop a few feet from her. Dust lifted over and around the car, and stole her breath. She coughed.

The wiry, short, and skinny lady threw open the car door. She jumped out and spoke before she could hear what Norma was saying. "—your mama."

Claire met her on the bottom step of the porch. The older lady reached for her and grabbed her in a hug. "Take me to your mama, kiddo."

She led the way to the barn. "The goat hurt her."

Within sight of Mama on the ground, Norma yelled. "Dotty?" She let go of Claire's hand and ran. At her side, she

32

bent on one knee and touched her cheek. "Sweetie, where does it hurt?"

She groaned and moved her head from side to side. "My hip."

Norma rested a hand on Mama's knee. "When you move it hurts?"

"Yes," she whispered. "Awful pain."

When she had fallen, her hair came loose from her ponytail. The black waves swept off the pillow the boys had given her and fanned over the dirt and leaves on the ground. Claire glanced at her brothers hovering near her head. Grayson's eyes shimmered with tears. Both squatted as close as they could get next to her. Liam's brow scrunched, and his lips puckered. He looked angry enough to spit and then he did—right over his shoulder and away from Mama. Claire knew him well. He was terrified.

She waved a hand at them. "We're going to help her. It'll be okay." But she worried. Poor Mama.

Norma stood, hands on her narrow hips. She blinked before speaking. "Here's the deal, Dot. I'm going to take you to the hospital in Wonder Pass. Not sure how to move you though." She nibbled her lip as she gazed at the boys.

Liam stirred, shuffling his feet. "What if we were to get the old army cot out of the service porch closet?"

Claire nodded. She knew from experience Liam had the best ideas in an emergency.

He took his hand out of his pocket and moved it about as he spoke. "We could haul her to the station wagon on the cot."

"Yes, that'll work." Norma patted his shoulder. "I'll drive your mama's car. We'll put down the back seat, and she can lie on soft blankets."

Claire clapped her hands once and gripped them together. "Let's do it. You boys—"

The boys popped upright and jogged away.

Norma squatted and caressed their patient's forehead. "Claire, where are the keys to the station wagon?"

She stared at Norma's back. Where had she seen them last? She snapped her fingers. "They're next to the phone in the living room."

"Got it." Norma strolled toward the house.

As Claire sat next to Mama and held her hand, Lolly came a few minutes later. "Sissy Pie, what's wrong?" She knelt next to their mother, hands on the ground, and peered into her face.

"I'll be okay, honey." She closed her eyes and jerked as though she had a stabbing pain. "I fell and hurt myself."

Claire leaned closer. "What can I do?"

"You're doing it, my sweet girl."

What did Mama mean? She couldn't stop her pain. She couldn't drive the station wagon. Her pretty face blurred through Claire's tears. "I haven't helped. I should have never let you milk Goat." She jabbed her forefinger at her chest. "It's my job." Her breath heaved in huge gulps.

"But I insisted, honey." She patted Claire's leg. "You are so good to organize and encourage." Her mouth rose at the edges in a hint of a smile but her breath caught.

She cringed and waited for Mama's gasps to stop.

Lolly patted her shoulder. "Does it hurt real bad?"

Her heart ached. "Of course she hurts."

Lolly slumped. "Poor, poor, Mama." Her eyes filled with tears as she gazed at her sister. "Oh, we have to hurry. Help Mama." She stared down at her pained face again and pulled the blanket higher on her chest.

She still held her hand as the fingers of her other hand caressed her cheek. "Do you want me to pray? Out loud?"

She blinked. "Please." Moisture trickled along the sides of her face.

Claire became aware at how brave Mama acted. If this were her, she would be sobbing like a baby.

Lolly bowed her head and Claire did the same, then prayed. "Dear God, please, please take away Mama's pain. Help us get her in the car. Have the doctors fix her hip. In Jesus' name. Amen."

"Amen."

A car motor purred from the front of the house and rumbled toward the barn. Norma turned the car around and eased the back of the tailgate to within a yard of where Mama lay.

Norma, Grayson, and Liam leapt from the car. They lifted the unfolded Army cot from the back of the station wagon and set it down on the ground alongside Mama.

"Claire, you and I will roll your mama onto her side away from the pain. Boys, you put the cot against her body and then we'll roll her onto the cot." She glanced at Mama. "Just in case you have broken your hip, Dot."

She studied Claire and her siblings. "This is going to cause more pain for your mama but keep going. Do not stop. On my count of three. One. Two. Three."

Grunts and groans escaped their lips. They got Mama on the edge of the cot but made it only inches toward the middle before she cried. "Oh, oh. Stop."

Norma patted her. "We're sorry, honey. Give us one more try, and we'll have you away from the edge." She counted again.

Claire's heart quivered at Mama's exclamations of, "Oh. Ow. Hurts."

This time, they settled her on the cot. And she sighed. The boys panted and rested hands on their knees. Claire blew a wayward curl off her mouth.

Mama whispered, "Please, let's go."

Even though her frame was slender, Claire wondered if she would be too much for their small group to carry. On another count of three the boys, Claire, and Norma lifted the cot and tugged it along. All the while, her face pinched and paled in what Claire knew was a painful experience. Within seconds, they reached the backside of the station wagon, lifted the cot higher, and slid her inside.

Norma slapped her hands together. "Liam, jump in the back with your mama. Keep her company."

He scrambled inside.

Claire, Grayson, and Lolly waved goodbye as Norma drove to the side of the house and disappeared. She breathed deeply, so relieved Mama was on her way to the hospital. Her breath froze in her lungs.

Feather. In the ruckus, she'd forgotten about the baby.

5

Claire sprinted toward the back of the house. As she approached the door, she stopped and cocked her ear to the side. Feather had sobbed so long his voice had gone hoarse. "Oh, no, oh, no, oh, no." Guilt nipped at her heels. She pushed open the pantry room door, skidded around the corner of the kitchen, and waved her arms to maintain her balance. Shame created heat on her cheeks. She ran through the living room and entered the hall—passing her bedroom on one side and her parents' on the other. Past the boys' room, she entered the small room Lolly and Feather shared. Beside Lolly's single bed sat a crib with a red-faced, tear-streaked baby whose face was covered in snot. His mouth opened wide with his garbled screams. He reached for her.

On the floor beneath the crib lay Laddie. When had he slipped away, and how did he get in the house? "Good boy, Laddie."

As Claire hurried to the baby, her chest tightened. For his need of her. Her neglect of him. "Hush now, Feather baby, don't cry." She lifted him high and over the crib bars. And he wrinkled his pug nose and slimed his fist through the snot. She hooked her finger and thumb around his wrist to stop a second swipe. "Let's get you clean, baby boy."

With his back against her chest, she carried him so she wasn't covered in snot too. He cried. "Ma. Ma."

Behind them, Laddie's toenails clicked on the wood floor.

He freed one hand and touched her face. "Yikes, Feather." She spit and sputtered and hurried to the bathroom, all the while she held him at arm's length. "Oh, mercy." She moaned over the mess he'd made.

She placed Feather in the empty tub. This way she could confine him so he wouldn't get too far. After she washed her face, she lifted his dirty shirt over his head, and it caught on his nose. "No," he squealed.

Claire stuck a finger in between his tee-shirt collar and the back of his head and lifted the shirt up and over her baby brother's head. He slapped at her arm. "Ma, Ma."

A long while later he was clean, and she planted him on her hip. "Are you ready to play?"

She carried him to the kitchen, but he kicked his heels and arched his back. A sure sign he wanted down. "Hey, hey. Don't hurt my belly." She grabbed his feet. "How about I fix you a bottle of milk?"

He bounced and squealed. "Bot, bot." His short, wide hands patted her shoulders. "Ma."

She kissed his forehead with a smack. "I love you, baby." When she reached the kitchen counter, she plopped him on his behind. "Feather, say, *Claire*."

He bobbed his body on the counter and clapped. "Ma."

A low chuckle rose from her chest, and she poked his stomach. "Okay. Say *Sis-sy*."

He leaned toward her and patted her cheeks. "See."

She fluttered her lashes. "Ah, baby boy, you said my name." For sure, she was excited at his first try.

Lolly entered the back door, mouth first. "Sissy Pie, where are you?"

She lifted the baby and hurried to the cupboard for a clean bottle and grabbed the milk from the refrigerator. She called out to let Lolly know she was in the kitchen. As she came into the pantry, Claire caught a glimpse of her sister. She appeared darker—*muddy*.

"Lolly Frances, why are you so dirty?" She sniffed. "Please tell me you weren't playing in the pig pen. Again." She narrowed her eyes for serious effect.

It worked. Her dirt-covered sibling bowed her head and fumbled her fingers together. Dried mud fell off of her and plopped on the floor.

She peered down near her sister's bare feet. "You're going to get the broom and sweep this up." When she didn't reply, Claire thought about having to wash another child in the tub. "What do you have to say for yourself?"

"Well." Lolly inhaled, her shoulders rising with her arched brows. "You see." She exhaled and blinked.

"Yes, I do see." Claire tapped her foot. "You stink like Blue, so I know you were in her pen." She tapped her muddy sister on the nose. "Since I don't have the time at the moment to clean you, march right outside and hose off."

Lashes a flutter, she inhaled again. "Okay, but can I take a bath too?"

Claire puckered her lips to the side and nibbled on the inside of her cheek. "Okay. Your hair won't come clean with a hose. Afterward, you will sweep up the dirt." She'd picked a very bad time to play in the pig's pen.

Instead of heading outside, Lolly moved closer and yanked on Claire's shirt. "Sissy Pie. When's Mama coming back?" Her face wrinkled with the question.

She bent to one knee and readjusted Feather on her other thigh. "Honey, I don't know."

Feather rocked. "Bot. Bot."

"Welp, but." Lolly's shoulders rose and lowered. "Will Daddy see about Mama?"

"You betcha. Now hose off and I'll start your bath." She glanced at the clock on the wall. Daddy would be home from work within four hours.

As Claire prepared Feather's bottle, her stomach grew queasy as though an army of ants had invaded and swarmed.

Would this injury cause Mama to have another breakdown like she had in Gallagher Springs?

6

"Mama needs surgery?" Claire's voice squeaked.

Norma sighed at the other end of the phone line. "Yes, darlin'. Your mama broke her hip when she fell."

She gripped the phone as tears threatened for the hundredth time that day. "Did the rock she landed on break her hip you think?" Her voice quivered.

"Sure could have and probably did." She cleared her throat. "I told the doctor she had fallen on a rock and let him know the size."

Unable to stifle a sob, she remembered Mama's fall, legs and arms flailing.

"Oh, honey," Norma said, "a fall like this is never any good."

Tears descended along her cheekbones. "I don't know what we're going to do." She didn't say what she really meant—that Mama was sensitive. She worried that this may affect her mind, and they'd need help.

"Now you listen to me, sweet pea. Ol' Norma's here to help." She paused a moment. "And I'll see if Mrs. Story will take turns staying at your place to babysit the little ones during school hours."

Feather's cries came from the kitchen, and Claire stared at the entryway. She sniffled and wiped the moisture on her cheeks with her sleeve. "I've got to go, Norma."

"All righty, kiddo. Don't you worry. We'll get it all figured out. I'll be driving the station wagon back to your place once your mama goes into surgery."

After she placed the phone in its cradle, she glanced Feather's way. In a hurry, she crossed through the formal dining room and into the kitchen. She tripped on a pan before reaching the baby where he had been playing in the pots and pans cupboard. She slapped her forehead. "Oh, Feather." What had he done now? Her lips trembled, but she refused to cry.

He still sobbed as he lifted his hand from where it was hidden behind a pan. Two of his little fingers were held fast under the metal clip of a mouse trap. "Ma, Ma."

"Oh, baby boy." Heart in her throat, she kneeled down. "How—?" She shook her head, unsure how to dislodge his purple, dented fingers. *Do something.* In her kneeling position, Claire opened the utensil drawer and grabbed a butter knife. She lightly held Feather's fingers so she could use the knife to pry on the edge of the trap between the wood and band of metal. Clinching her teeth, she twisted. When there was space, she pulled his fingers from the trap.

As the trap fell to the floor, he waved his hand. "Ow, ow, ow, Ma, Ma."

She swung him up and on her hip and spoke in a soothing tone. She placed a bowl under the faucet and ran cold water. His chest shuttered with his weeping, but when she placed his hand in the water he sucked in a breath. "Poor baby. We'll fix you right up."

The phone rang at the same time Grayson and Lolly entered the kitchen.

"Grayson, get the phone."

He raced around the wood cookstove and entered the living room. In a few moments, he said, "Hello? Uh-huh. Okay."

She shushed the baby and hurried toward her brother.

"I'll ask her." Grayson rested the receiver on his shoulder. "Norma says she won't leave until Daddy gets to the hospital."

"Tell her thank you." She retraced her steps back to the kitchen.

After he said goodbye to Norma, all Claire thought about was how Mama would need help when she came home. She dunked Feather's hand back in the cold water. She dreaded the days of disorder.

When an idea hit, she raised her chin and stared at the backyard through the window above the sink. They really needed Grandma Neecy now. And if she came, Belinda would come with her.

If only Belinda had a phone.

She motioned for her little brother. "Come hold Feather while he soaks his fingers."

He peered into the bowl of water. "What happened?"

"Mousetrap." She moved to get a chair and water dripped off of the baby's hand as she carried him along. "Here." She tugged the chair to the sink. "Get on your knees.

Now I'll put Feather in front of you. Hold his hand in the water like this."

"What are you gonna do?"

"I have a letter to write."

~^~^~

Dear Grandma Neecy,

Mama's in bad shape. She broke her hip bone when she fell off a stool. She is in the hospital and will have surgery. Please, please would you come to live with us while Mama heals? I do not know for how long, but we need you.

I would ask my grandparents, but they have taken a long vacation to Alasca (I think I spelled that right, but it looks funny) to visit my uncle. They won't be back until November.

Claire tapped her pencil against her bottom lip, thinking about what to say so Grandma Neecy would come. *Oh, I know.* She pressed her pencil to the light blue stationery page.

When Daddy is done fixing up the apartment you and Belinda will have your own place.

How she wanted to convince Grandma Neecy to live with them forever. If they came, she would ask Grandma Neecy about that. She bowed her head over the letter and continued.

You know how sensitive Mama can be. I cannot do this by myself, and I cannot miss too much school. Please write to me or call me at 2772 to let me know if you can come. Love, Claire

~√√~

Daddy's pickup made the sound Claire always listened for—a *bum, bum da, bum, da* as he geared down Anderson Hill on the Redwood Highway in front of their property. She grabbed Feather, and she, Grayson, and Lolly sprinted through the open front door to greet him. She knew her news would cause Daddy to ask a dozen questions about Mama's injury.

He drove on the circle drive where withered daisy petals ringed and had fallen like snow with the summer heat. He stopped the pickup in front of them.

He turned off the engine, and Claire raced to the driver's door. Her siblings pushed against her back. Everyone talked at once, which seemed to cause Daddy's face to go blank. She threw out a *shush* over her shoulder at her siblings' chatter.

"Whoa." Daddy raised a hand. "What's this about, Claire?"

She gulped down a sob and blurted. "Mama's in the hospital."

The whites around his nut brown irises grew and appeared brighter against his dusty face. "What?" His bushy brows crept together like two caterpillars touching noses. Then he asked a question in Portuguese. A sure sign he was upset, and she wouldn't correct him that she didn't understand his words.

"Mama fell and broke her hip."

With his thumb and forefinger, her father pinched his brows. He got out of the pickup and groaned another foreign word. "I mean how?"

She filled him in as he sighed and shuffled his boots. At one point, he took a fidgety Feather who jabbered nonsense while he reached for him. He shook his head. "I told your mama it was your job to milk the goat."

She then gave him the message from Norma. When she finished, he rested the baby on the top of the open pickup door and gazed in the direction he'd need to travel.

Was he thinking about the forty-five minute drive after being awake since four a.m.?

Lolly tugged on his belt. "Daddy, you going to see Mama at the hospital?"

Without a glance at her, he placed the baby into Claire's arms and hurried into the house. Not a minute later, he came back outside and descended the porch steps. His black hair shined, curls damp. His face was no longer covered in a fine powder but washed clean. Claire stared at his blushed face, filled with emotion and ready to erupt.

"Take care of the kids. I've got to see about your mama." He swung onto the seat and shut the door. Out the open window, he waved a hand at her. "I'll be in late tonight." He started the engine and everyone moved away. The pickup inched forward with a lurch.

Hands on her hips, Claire waited until the vehicle slowed at the end of the driveway. Daddy gunned the engine, and he disappeared down the highway.

"Welp." Grayson shuffled at her side. "What'll we do now?"

Go into the house, run to my room, and cry. She readjusted the baby in her arms and took the four steps onto the porch. "Fix supper."

Grayson moved his hands about as he talked. "Don't we have plenty of your blackberry stew left over?"

Ah, she forgot about the berry delight in a big pot in the refrigerator. "Oh. We don't have to fix anything. Do you guys want it cold? Or should I heat it up?"

Everyone yelled, "Heated."

Lolly got into step with her. "Can I help, Sissy Pie?"

"Yes." She rubbed a spot of dirt off the baby's cheek. "You can play with Feather."

Grayson pushed the door open wider and stepped inside. "Will you make waffles too?"

Lolly clapped and stomped her feet in place. "Yes. Please?"

Feather patted his palms together. "See, See."

She kissed the baby on the forehead and leaned near her brother. "The berry stew will fill our bellies and cheer us." Besides, she was worn to a stub like the end of a used pencil.

Grayson rushed to the counter and climbed on it. "I'll set the table." As he announced this, he opened a top cupboard and pulled out their mismatched and chipped bowls.

He always helped her when she needed it most. She bent to one knee and retrieved a medium-sized pan. In no time, she had the stew warmed.

She turned her back to her siblings to wash her hands at the kitchen sink. Lolly howled loud enough to curl her toes. She frowned and faced her little sister. "What's wrong?"

"Grayson took my chair."

He crossed his arms and leveled her with his meanest expression. She always wanted to laugh because it wasn't more than the scrunch of his brows. She swore he managed a bit of a lift to the sides of his mouth as though he thought about smiling. His frown wobbled. "Your name's on this chair?"

Lolly stuck her tongue out at him.

With a huff of her breath, she settled her sister on one of the other chairs. "It's time to eat, not fight, you two."

Claire sat in her chair and blew out a long breath. She didn't need one more problem in an already upside down day.

~∧~∧~

Laddie dog barked, and the noise woke Claire. All was dark but was not quiet.

The front door, next to her bedroom, opened. Daddy's voice *shhh*ed and boots scuffed, which made her eyes open with a zing. Once the quiet returned, she snuggled deeper under the covers. Feather squirmed next to her and whimpered. She whispered. "Go back to sleep, baby boy."

It seemed like only minutes that she awoke again, but this time to the scent of coffee. She patted the spot where Feather slept, then bolted upright. Empty. "Where's the baby?" She crawled to the end of the bed and peered at the floor. No baby.

She kicked off the covers and followed her nose to the kitchen entry and stopped. In his highchair, Feather ate. No. Actually, he wore his cream of wheat cereal. He raised his cereal-encrusted brows and made eye contact with her, and then he wrinkled his nose. "See, See."

Her shoulders relaxed as she approached him. "There you are, you little stink." She laughed at the sight of him.

He grinned, exposing his few baby teeth and pounded a spoon in his plastic bowl. More cereal *splat, splatt*ed on his forehead. His hair. He giggled. She finger-scooped mush off of him. "Yes, I'm Sissy." She touched his chest. "Who are you?"

He patted her hand with his pudgy, messy one. "You."

She grabbed a wet cloth from the sink and wiped his face. "No." She tapped his chest. "Feather."

"Good morning, Claire." She lifted her gaze to Daddy. The blood vessels in the whites of his eyes were stark around his pupils.

She dropped the washcloth on the baby's highchair tray and turned to hug him around the waist. "You look so tired." She craned her neck. "How's Mama? How did the surgery go?"

He patted her arm. "Surgery is scheduled for this afternoon."

"Oh." She snuggled deeper into his chest, seeking the beat of his heart. What else was there to say? They both had to wait to see how Mama did in surgery and then how she'd do once she came home.

7

Claire swished her arms at her siblings. "Move out of the way, kids. Let them through."

Eight days after surgery, Mama came home. She stayed at the hospital longer, Daddy had told her, because of the extra needed rest before she returned to her big family.

While her mother was gone, Claire had some help. Norma and their elderly neighbor, Mrs. Story, cooked their evening meals. She did almost everything else. She cared for her siblings, did the laundry, and milked Goat. The boys did outdoor chores when they got home from school. Their pig, Blue, and their few chickens needed care. At night, the boys cleaned the kitchen while Claire bathed Lolly and Feather.

Truth be told, she didn't miss the tension of dealing with the Lavender Girls at school. She did get to talk on the phone with Lizbeth. And Claire had arranged to have her school work sent home so she wouldn't fall too far behind. A girl named Lorene brought it to Liam on the school bus each day.

Mama and Daddy made their way to the steps and into the house. Claire noticed two things as her mother used one crutch with Daddy bearing her weight on her injured hip side. Her clothes hung on her thin frame, reminding Claire of the scarecrow her father had made to keep birds out of their corn field. The smudges under her eyes unleashed memories of what she looked like after Feather's birth.

"Claire," Daddy's voice jarred her, "grab the pillows off your mama's bed and bring them to the sofa."

"Yes, sir." She raced to her parents' room, gathered two pillows, and placed them on the sofa.

"*Umph.*" Mama's breath swished a loud exhale as Daddy helped her lie down. "Thank you, my sweet girl." She leaned her head against the pillows. "I'm exhausted."

Oh, she didn't want to hear this. She had slept all the time after Feather's birth. Would she do that again?

Mama opened one eye. "Where's my baby?"

Claire knelt next to the sofa, afraid her weight on the couch would hurt Mama. "He's napping."

Her lips parted as if to smile. But she grimaced instead.

Daddy held a quilt in his arms and covered Mama from feet to chin. He backed away. "Okay, let her sleep."

Her brothers were near the front door. "We're headed to the target practice range with our slingshots, Claire."

She got off her knees and met them on the porch. "Be back in an hour for super." She was relieved the neighbors would continue to bring meals for another week.

As was his habit, Liam puckered his lips and whistle-tweeted softly to show he understood. He tried to teach her how to whistle like that but she always failed.

As she went back into the living room, two emotional sounds from her parents hit her ears with a smack. Mama's cries. Daddy begging her to stay calm and rest.

She trembled as Mama's sobs grew louder, and Claire checked on the baby in her room. She peered down at him, his breathing calm as the trickle of their creek in late spring. Without a second thought, she shut her door to deaden the noise of her parents and lay on her bed next to Feather.

Her mind grew full of sleep, until a thought popped open her eyes. Belinda's Grandma should have received her letter by now. Would they come? What else could she do to convince them to come live with them? In a quiet voice, she prayed. "Lord, please, we need them. In Jesus' name, I ask. Amen."

The click of her door woke her. Her brothers were at her side of the bed. She knew this without opening her eyes—the smell of dirt assaulted her nose. The mattress sank, moving her toward them. "Claire?" Liam's eyes were round as his bull's eye targets he pings with his sling shot and rocks. "Daddy told us to be real quiet. I guess Mama's upset. Lots of pain."

She tapped her lips. "Shh. Don't wake the baby." Her lids closed against Liam's frightened features. "I know. I heard."

A hand rested on her shoulder. Grayson. Her heart ached for their fears of the past coming full circle. "What are we gonna do? Is Mama gonna be like when Feather was born?"

Liam made a noise like sucking air through his teeth. "We need help. Unless you stay home from school some more."

"I do have to stay home for a while longer, but I've written a letter."

Liam sat next to Grayson on the side of the bed. "To who?"

She raised the upper half of her body and leaned on her elbow. "Don't tell Daddy. I need to talk to him first. But I wrote to Grandma Neecy, guys." Both of the boys tilted their heads. "To ask her and Belinda to come live with us until Mama's hip is healed."

"You didn't ask Daddy first?"

Grayson shook his head. "Uh-oh."

"No." She frowned and sat upright. "I haven't had five minutes with him. So, I made an important decision. Besides, he likes Grandma Neecy, and if she says she's coming, I think he'll be relieved." She smiled. "He knows she calms Mama's nerves."

Liam snorted and pushed his too long bangs from his forehead. "You are so sure of yourself. He could get pretty sore at you, you know."

"Yeah." Grayson drew out the word as though he was in awe. "He'll even talk Portuguese in a growly voice."

Feather whimpered.

She lifted the baby to her chest and patted his back. "Daddy trusts me to help, so that's what I'm doing. Besides, I don't want to miss too much school." Not that she missed the snooty Lavender Girls.

Liam picked a scab off his elbow, and she wrinkled her nose. He pinned her with a stare. "I don't blame you. School is fun being with my old friends."

"Yeah," Grayson laughed. "I missed my buddies."

She scooted to the bed's edge and stood. "Let's set the table before our meal comes. Who wants to babysit Feather?"

"I'll take him." Grayson reached for the baby. "He and I are buddies too."

She handed Feather over, and she and Liam walked toward the kitchen. When she passed partway through the living room, she stilled. Lolly lay asleep at the space below Mama's feet.

Another dull ache churned in her chest for all of them. *Please, God. Bring Grandma Neecy to us.*

~∧~∧~

Mama had been home for two days, and Claire still stayed home to help.

When Liam arrived from school, he brought in the mail. He stood next to her where she was washing lunch dishes. "Here." He laid an envelope on the counter. "I think you've been waiting for this." His expression held a hopeful, soft look. The worry lines had eased. Even at eleven, he wore creases on his forehead like that of a thirty-year-old.

Eager, she rinsed and dried her hands, all the while peeking at the return address. She opened the letter and read aloud as she and her brothers bunched into a huddle.

"Dear Claire,

"I was sad to hear yer poor mama is having another bout of trouble. Of course me and Belinda would be most willing to come live with y'all and help with yer family.

56

Nothing here holds us. My daughter is a movie star in Hollywood. Making her first movie.

"Belinda has been helping me pack to come live in Oregon. We will bring Bossy. We will need her milk at yer house. Like we do here. Big Red will haul Bossy in the back of his pickup.

"The Good Lord willing, look for us to come on Tuesday evening."

Claire gasped.

Liam's hand shot out and grabbed the letter. He stared at it. "Oh, boy." He scratched a spot on his neck. "You're in trouble now." He grinned. "But I'm not sorry you wrote Grandma Neecy."

She could barely put together two words, but her excitement won. "She's, she's coming." She clasped her hands together. "Thank you, dear Lord, thank you."

"Yeah, but—," Grayson waved a hand, "where they gonna sleep?"

Claire's heart double-thumped. Oh, dear. She'd promised them the room in the shop. Well, she'd just have to give them her bed instead. She swiveled her gaze to the wall clock. "Daddy will be home soon, and I've got to change my sheets."

Since Mama had been pretty much bedridden, he had been coming home a couple hours earlier to help. And Norma assisted with her needs several times a day.

She had a little time to change the sheets. She needed to show Daddy she was ready for Grandma Neecy and Belinda.

~∧~∧~

Daddy's eyes bugged like a bullfrog's. "You did what?"

Uh-oh.

He licked his lips and inhaled. "Claire. I can't believe this. Writing and telling Mrs. Wolf she and Belinda could come live with us?" He bowed his head and shook it twice.

She stared at her toes and bit on a ragged fingernail. She really thought he'd be relieved.

"Well?" His voice still not happy. "What else should I know?" He lifted her chin with his finger. "Speak." Sweat dotted his forehead and the space between his caterpillar brows narrowed.

She heaved a sigh. "Um, well, I told Grandma Neecy she and Belinda could live in the apartment attached to your shop." She flinched. "When you get it built."

"You didn't." He arched his neck backward. "Oh, for—" a string of Portuguese words flew from between his lips. His face flushed as red as a garden beet.

Unable to pull her gaze from him, her muscles twitched. She couldn't bear to tell the rest. But she wouldn't lie. Besides, he'd find out soon enough. "There's one more thing."

He gasped and glanced at her brothers who stood in a corner of the living room. "Did you two know about this?"

One shook his head no and the other, yes.

Daddy raised his hands and settled them on his jean-clad hips. "What else, Claire?"

"Before I tell you, please, remember how calming Grandma Neecy was for Mama back at Gallagher Springs?"

He wiped the sweat from his forehead with his hanky. "She was a lifesaver."

She folded her hands as though to pray. "She can be that lifesaver again, Daddy. We need her. I can't miss anymore school and our neighbors have been helping for two weeks now."

He stared at the floor. "I see your point, but you should have discussed this with me first, Claire."

"I'm sorry. You're right." She dug the letter from her pants pocket and opened it. "Here's the other thing, Daddy." She read, "Look for us on Tuesday evening."

"Next week Tuesday?" his expression eased. "Whew. That gives me time to work on their apartment."

Claire sucked in her bottom lip and nibbled.

"Oh, no. You mean today, Tuesday."

It wasn't a question, so she blinked.

Now his face flushed to near purple.

Oh boy. She inhaled a deep breath and stilled herself against the onslaught of Portuguese.

She fumbled the letter between her fingers. She had to remind herself that he never stayed upset for long.

Grayson jerked on her plaid shirt. "Don't forget about the cow."

Claire winced.

Daddy leaned in close to her. "Coooowww?" His garlic breath hot on her cheeks.

She lifted her palms. "They have to bring Bossy." She fluttered her lashes, hoping he would go easy on this tiny bit of information.

"How?" He swallowed. "Who's bringing it? Because surely Mrs. Wolf can't do that by herself."

Claire knew what she said next would help him get used to this whole idea even better. She grinned. "Big Red."

The phone rang and interrupted their conversation. She scurried over to answer on the fourth ring. "Hello? Yes. Hi! You're less than an hour from our place. I'll give Daddy the phone, and he'll explain." She held out the phone for him. "It's Grandma Neecy. She's in Wonder Pass."

He patted his forehead again with the hanky, said a single word in Portuguese, and spoke into the phone. "Mrs. Wolf? Big Red is with you? Okay. You'll travel south on Redwood Highway."

Claire didn't need to hear anymore. She entered the kitchen to get a drink of water for her dry-as-dirt throat. The conversation with her father hadn't gone too bad. She leaned against the counter and drank and thought.

Moments later, Daddy walked into the kitchen, his expression calm. "I didn't believe you when you said Big Red was coming with them. I guess it will be good to see my ol' buddy." He crossed his arms. "What breed of cow is Bossy?"

She shrugged. I don't know. All I know is she's light brown and not too big."

"Ah, good. She's probably a Jersey. They're one of the smaller breeds and good natured."

Claire placed the empty glass in the sink. "Don't you think it will be nice to have lots of fresh milk? What we get from Goat is never enough. And remember you told me you'd buy me a milk cow once we came back from Gallagher Springs." She didn't mean to this time, but her lashes fluttered.

He tipped his chin and didn't bat an eye. "You know I couldn't pass up a free milking goat." He rubbed his temple. "You've made so much work for me. I need to get the barn ready to house a cow, although I won't need to make a large enclosure for a Jersey. And I need to finish the apartment sooner rather than later."

She stared at a rip in their checkerboard linoleum.

He spoke again and she looked up. "What?"

He leaned in. "Have you figured out the sleeping arrangements? Because I don't have the time."

"I'll sleep on the couch and give Grandma Neecy and Belinda my bed." She touched his shoulder. "You'll see, Daddy, this is going to work."

"Of course." He stared through the kitchen window. His brows scrunched and wiggled in half frowns. Was he seeing into the past? "That kind old woman knows how to handle your mama."

She patted his arm. "I had to do something. I can't miss anymore school."

He stuffed his hands into his pockets and lowered his gaze. "I know, ClaireBear."

Her limbs relaxed at her nickname.

Daddy had accepted her take-charge decision.

8

Claire hurried to prepare her bedroom for company. She stored the clutter in a box and smashed her dresses over to make room in her closet for their clothes. She swept and mopped the floors, made a bed for herself in the corner of the room, and laid a stack of blankets and one pillow on the end of the sofa in the living room for Big Red.

Daddy and the boys left to lay fresh straw down for Bossy in the barn and to make any repairs needed to hold the cow. Later, as she prepared a large pot of stew and cornbread, her father washed his hands at the kitchen sink. "I'll build an enclosed stall for Bossy this weekend. She can sleep in there at night, and it will double as a milking area."

The last potato was diced and added to the carrots and chunks of venison simmering in the pot. "Thanks, Daddy." She jumped as someone knocked on the front door. She wiped her hands on a dish towel and hurried from the kitchen. Her mind buzzed. Must be Belinda and Grandma Neecy.

Except for Mama resting in her room, the entire Monteiro family met their friends on the front porch. The girls squealed and stepped into a rocking embrace, with Claire's cheek nestled against Belinda's upper arm.

Her friend's hair reached halfway down her back now, no longer just below her shoulders. She styled it away from her face with barrettes holding it back. Also, her nails were a bit longer, with clear nail polish making them shimmer. Claire made a mental note to later praise Belinda for the improvement her appearance.

Her own nails were still short and ragged from her constant nail biting. It didn't matter. Belinda and Grandma Neecy had come and that was what counted.

After supper, the men moved to the living room with their cups of coffee. Liam tried to follow, but Claire yanked his arm. "Oh, no, you don't. Clean off the table. Grayson, you start the dishes."

Grandma Neecy interrupted. "I'll help here, Claire."

She squeezed the old woman's hand. "No, ma'am. You and Belinda need to rest. Settle into my room. Take a shower if you want." She furrowed her brows at her brothers. "We've got this under control, right boys?"

Liam's arms hung at his sides as he rubbed his index fingers and thumbs together. Grayson already headed to the kitchen for his chore.

Lolly tugged on her sister's shirt. She had put on Claire's apron and was smiling, hands on hips. "What about me, Sissy Pie?"

She pursed her lips to keep down the laughter. Her little sister loved to act grown up. But any time anyone laughed at something she said, she thought people were being mean. "You clean Feather's face and hands. When you're done, I'll help him out of his high chair, and then you can dress him for bed." She took a step toward the kitchen but thought of something else. "Would you lie down with Feather on your bed? See if you can sing him to sleep?"

"Yes, Sissy." She nodded her head in a flare of drama.

Claire angled her face away and chuckled. Even Lolly was excited about their company.

Belinda touched her elbow. "We'll take showers and unpack. Thanks for givin' us your bed."

"I still can't believe you are here."

"Me, either, little buddy. Oops." She slapped a hand over her mouth. "I forgot. Ya don't like me callin' ya—that. The LB name."

She intertwined her fingers with Belinda's and swayed back and forth. "I've changed my mind—it's the special name you gave to me. Besides, I've missed you." She drew closer to her friend. "You're still head and shoulders taller than me. I even grew since I last saw you in June."

"Aw. I couldn't ask for a better buddy." She punched Claire's front shoulder. Even though she understood Belinda meant it as soft, she wobbled. Belinda turned toward the bathroom where a hot shower waited. "I best get to it."

She marveled at her giant of a friend as she walked across the living room floor. She belonged.

~∧~∧~

The siblings hurried through kitchen clean up. Later on, kids met with the grownups in the living room where Mama sat with Feather at her feet. Claire guessed her sister couldn't get him to sleep. She checked the clock on the dining room wall. It was late at nine o'clock, but the visiting continued. And her lips stayed creased up at the corners.

Showered and dressed in a simple shift, Belinda sat with Claire on the living room floor and scratched behind Laddie's ear as he lay next to her. The two friends talked in low voices, while conversations around them dimmed.

"I sure enough missed ya, and Grandma was tickled when ya wrote to tell us ya needed our help." She gasped and whispered. "Not tickled about your ma. Just that ya thought of us."

"I had to, you know?" She slid a glance toward Mama. Her fingers twitched and fumbled with the hem of Feather's pajama top. Did anyone else see? She wouldn't look around, just in case. Instead, she drew closer to her friend until their elbows touched. "She's nervous."

"Sure enough." Belinda's solemn expression mirrored her anxious heart. But. Grandma Neecy had come to the rescue.

Big Red laughed, causing Mama to jump.

Claire unfolded her crossed legs, rose, and leaned near Mama's ear. "Isn't it bedtime for you and Feather?"

Her eyes softened, making them droopy. "Yes, I'm tired and my hip hurts."

She reached for Feather. He stretched out his arms to her. "See, See." She swung him onto her hip and kissed his cheek with a loud *smack.*

Belinda hurried over and helped Mama stand, even though she had crutches. "You're light as a feather, Mrs. M."

Feather jerked his head and patted his chest. "Me, me."

Belinda giggled. "Yeah. You're Feather."

With help, Mama walked little steps down the wide hall toward her room. Claire followed with the baby.

Behind them, Grandma Neecy yoo-hooed. "Good night, Dotty."

Mama came to a halt. "Same to you, Neecy. Are you staying for long?"

Claire stiffened, at the same moment she tightened her grip on Feather. She had forgotten a detail.

A critical one.

Would Grandma Neecy say too much? If she did, Mama would know she'd invited them to stay a while. And she would know why. That would surely make her mother feel guilty about not being able to take care of her own family.

Would that push Mama over the edge?

It was all Claire's fault.

~∧~∧~

Grandma Neecy stood. "Well, Dotty, why don't we play it by ear?" She moseyed toward her. "Would that be okay with ya, darlin'?"

"Of course." The whisper breezed through Mama's lips like a sigh of relief. "I love your company, Neecy."

The old woman took Mama's other side and walked. "We'll see ya in the morning, hon. Please, sleep as long as ya need."

She sniffled. A tear escaped and trickled along her cheek. "I'm grateful you are here, Neecy."

Mama's figure grew blurry as Claire waited.

Grandma Neecy's pudgy arm wrapped across Mama's shoulders. She patted. "I'll get breakfast and get the youngin's off to school."

"Thank you." Mama swiped a shaky hand across her cheek and continued with careful movements toward her bedroom.

Above Mama's head, Belinda winked as in "good job, little buddy." Claire followed them, much relieved that Grandma Neecy seemed to understand.

Once they settled Mama and Feather in the bed, Mama moved her hand in circles on his back. "Claire, please come in about fifteen minutes and take the baby to his bed. By then, he should be asleep."

"Okay. And if he gets fussy in his own bed later, he can sleep with me." She didn't tell Mama that for now the floor was her bed. It was too late for her to suggest changes to the sleeping arrangements.

She slipped into her room and snuggled under quilts on the floor. Minutes later, Belinda plopped next to her. "Grandma saved your bacon." She giggled.

She sat up and readjusted the covers. "I was starting to sweat there for a moment. I had forgotten Mama knew nothing about my letter to you guys. At least she's never said anything, so I guess Daddy didn't tell her." She yawned. "I should have known Grandma Neecy would figure it out."

"I wondered for a second myself."

When the adults grew quiet in the living room, Claire cupped her hand around her mouth and whispered in her ear, "I have to tell you something, and I'm not joking."

Leaning back, Belinda cocked her one good brow as the other couldn't move. It was scarred along with that side of her face from a car accident.

She wiggled her index finger for Belinda to once again come closer. "Wendy Lavender and Kaye Tyner are already making trouble for me at school."

"No way."

"Honest."

"That's spooky. Why would they follow ya to your school?"

Claire crossed her arms on her raised knees and let go a buzz sigh. "There's a new road being built for a shorter route to the coast south of here. My dad's blasting again through another mountain to build—"

"Another tunnel." Belinda slapped her leg. "I'll be, hot diggity. We're still not free of those bullies." She puckered her mouth into a knot. "Disprickable."

Claire giggled behind her hand.

"What?" Her lips wobbled. "Did I say a funny?"

"I think you meant to say despicable. It means shameful."

"Despicable."

"I thought I was seeing things when I first spotted Kaye at school."

"Oh?"

"Kaye said she *accidently* stumbled into my locker door. The door smacked me in the head."

"Oh, dear Lord. I'm sorry." She pressed a hand on Claire's shoulder. "We'll stick by each other like never before."

"Of course." She waved a hand. "Tomorrow, you'll meet my other best friend, Lizbeth." Belinda's brow rose. "No worries. You'll really like her. I've already filled her in on the Lavender Girls too."

"Good. Three's better than two against those hoity-toity girls."

Later, in the dark of her room, Claire grinned. She, Belinda, and Lizbeth would be a force to reckon with against the bullies. She closed her eyes. Another thought and her eyes pinged open.

What if the Lavender Girls did steal Lizbeth's friendship like they attempted to steal her from Belinda back in Gallagher Springs? She clenched her teeth—her sleep had fled.

9

"I have a surprise." Lizbeth stared past Claire. She tugged on Belinda's hand and guided her to stand by her other friend. "This is Belinda Cruz. She's living with us for now. Belinda, this is Lizbeth Meyer." The two girls gazed at each other.

After a pause, all three talked at once. Soon, and with Claire in the middle, the girls locked arms. They walked toward the school's double doors.

"What do we have here?"

She had dreaded that voice before Belinda came. But no more.

Kaye popped a big bubble with her chewing gum. "Never thought I'd see you again, Cruz."

Wendy snapped her gum as she stood next to Kaye.

Claire sliced a hand through the air. "Enough."

Belinda stared down her nose at Kaye.

"And so," she persisted, "it would be a good idea for you to stop the bullying." She poked a finger in their direction. Did the Lavenders just flinch? She could only hope.

Belinda cocked a thumb at their tight band of three. "Don't. Mess. With. Us."

The bell rang. The threesome resumed their walk. Lizbeth paused and glanced at them. "Don't you care what they think of you two?"

Belinda sniffed. "It's none of my business what people think of me. I know what's right and I know what's wrong and they're all wrong."

Claire motioned a hand for the girls to come closer. "Let's form our own group."

Lizbeth frowned. "Why?"

"To protect ourselves against those uppity girls. Not sure what we should call ourselves though. Let's discuss it during first break and at lunch."

"Okay."

"We need to get to class." Lizbeth grabbed their hands.

Kaye and Wendy moved past the girls, but not before Kaye brushed a shoulder against Claire's. Lizbeth grabbed her as she missed a step. "Whoa. They don't listen, do they?"

Belinda's eyes became mere slits. "Ya ain't seen nothin' yet."

Steady now on her feet, she retucked her sack lunch under her arm. "This school year is starting out rough."

~∧~∧~

The girls spent their first break slouched against a pine tree behind the gym. Thrill raced along Claire's spine as they discussed what to name their group.

Meanwhile, Belinda sucked on a lollipop. "How about Rebel Girls?"

Claire and Lizbeth glanced at each other. Lizbeth twirled a cross at the end of her long necklace. "How about Truth Revivers?"

"Revivers?" She tested the word on her tongue.

"Sounds too holier-than-thou."

"Well." Lizbeth stared down at her clasped hands in front of her. "If we're going to be a nice club and not mean like the Lavender Girls, wouldn't it fit?"

"Ya see, it also sounds like an old ladies club."

"Oh."

Claire nodded. "How about something with "girls" in it. Like the Lavender Girls have?"

"Sounds like a good start." Lizbeth's chin lifted, and Claire knew her feelings weren't hurt.

She nibbled on a ragged finger nail. "How about the Winner Girls Club. The Friendly Girls Club. The Happy Girls Club. The—"

"Stop." Belinda shook the lollipop. "Corny, Claire, real corny."

With her hands on her hips, she sighed. "You're hard to please."

"I just know what doesn't sound right."

Lizbeth gave an eye roll, but remained silent.

Belinda snapped her fingers. "I've got it. The Warrior Girls Club."

"What?" Lizbeth's eyes popped wide open. "That sounds so mean. Unladylike even."

"Yeah? What's yer point?"

Claire waved her palms. "Wait. Wait. Why don't we use a synonym for warrior, so it sounds more feminine?"

Belinda puffed out her cheeks. "What's a synonym?"

Before Claire answered, Wendy and Kaye strolled over to them. "What are we doing, girls?"

As if they were a part of their friendship.

Belinda stepped closer to them. "Don't start in on us 'cause we may be nice, but we won't take any guff." She ended her words with a hard dip of her chin.

Wendy drew closer. "Really, Cruz?" A devilish smirk grew on her watermelon-pink painted lips. She opened her mouth—

Claire crossed her arms and stepped between them. "You really don't want to do this."

Wendy crossed her arms like a copycat and got nose to nose with her. "And why not, ClaireLee?"

"I don't go by my full name anymore. Just Claire."

Kaye interrupted. "And why is that, Sissy Pie?" She guffawed. "Such a stupid, childish name. Your sister is a dork."

All common sense flew from Claire's brain. She smashed into Kaye and she stumbled.

"Stop." Lizbeth grabbed her arms and pulled. All the way into the building, down the hall, and into the girls' restroom. Behind the closed door, she faced Claire. Her eyes filled with what? Disappointment? Pity? "What's gotten in to you?"

Claire's heart pumped as though she'd run a mile around the school track, her breath gushed. "You do . . . not know . . . what . . . Belinda and I went through with those girls. Especially Kaye. She is hateful, mean, and I'd like to punch her in the face."

She gasped. "Oh, Claire, that's too horrid. And you know revenge is sinful."

"Wait and see. You'll be sick of them way before they go back home to Boston."

She whispered. "But Claire. I've known you since we were nine. You've never acted like this. Besides, violence never, ever solves problems." She touched her friend's arms. "You know this. I believe in you. Always will."

"They've ruined another school year. For me. For Belinda." She swallowed. "I've developed such a temper. Life's been, well . . ." She stared at her. "I've not told you everything." She wiped at her nose.

The door opened. "I took care of her for ya, little buddy." She brushed her palms together as though slapping off dirt.

Lizbeth sucked in a breath and leaned back. "What did you do?"

She raised one hand. "No, it's not what ya think. I didn't rough her up or anything." She grinned. "I sure wanted to. But it's like this. I told Miss Tyner if she doesn't mind her own affairs, I'd get a rumor goin' about how she embarrassed herself at the awards ceremony at Gallagher Springs Elementary. How her daddy hauled her off by the arm."

Claire cleared her throat. "That would not be a rumor but a fact." Her belly churned. "How is that going to make her leave us alone?"

"I'm thinkin', Claire, you've lived around here a lotta years. Everyone knows your family. Am I right?"

She nodded and swiped at the moisture in her eyes.

"Well, then, kids won't like Kaye Tyner when they hear how she hurt your mama's feelings. How your mama was humiliated."

The school bell rang. As well as a warning bell dinging in Claire's head. They had to keep Mama's secret. She would make sure Belinda understood.

All three girls left the bathroom and walked to class. When they met Wendy and Kaye in the hall, Lizbeth and Belinda pressed closer to Claire who was in the middle. Were her friends protecting her from the Lavender Girls or the other way around?

~∧~∧~

After school, Lizbeth took her bus south to Cavern Junction. Belinda and Claire rode their bus north to Selmac.

Claire nibbled on a fingernail and slumped in the seat.

"Hey, little buddy. What's ailin' ya?"

"I just hate this. We're together again, but the Lavender Girls—"

"Not unless we let them bother us." She quirked the corner of her mouth.

"I know you're right." Her mind begged for some of her friend's confidence. "I'm glad we have you to help us."

"Little buddy, Grandma tells me that when we have troubles we should count our blessings."

"Count my blessings … I try, but I always forget." She slumped lower into the leather seat. "It's like I get stuck in the unhappy thoughts." Could she find something good out of the recent conflict? She remembered a word Belinda had said earlier. "I think you said part of the name for our group."

"Huh?" She crossed her eyes. Her way, Claire knew, for being silly.

"At school you said the word 'guff'."

She narrowed her eyes, saying nothing for a long moment. "Oh, yeah, to Kaye."

Claire straightened in the bus seat. "How about the Guff Girls?"

"Ahhh." She studied the bus ceiling. "Not sure."

The bus slowed to a stop and the brakes squeaked. They were at their driveway, and the two friends followed the boys off the bus. Her steps matched Belinda's as the boys ran ahead. "So what do you think?"

"About the name? What if we called ourselves the GG Club? That way the Lavender Girls don't know the full name."

Would that make the mean girls even meaner? Because after today, she no longer trusted herself. She knew better—just like Lizbeth said. She should not give an eye for an eye. But what could she do instead?

10

After the stroll along the driveway, the girls entered the kitchen and found the boys already at the table. They munched on what appeared to be homemade donuts. It seemed impossible to hope Mama had made them, especially in her condition. At the sink Grandma Neecy peeled potatoes while Mama cut them into flat, round slices. The two women chatted like old friends.

Claire's heart warmed at the sight of Mama's crutches leaning against the counter. She seemed normal and happy in the kitchen instead of resting on the sofa. Overcome with emotion, she reached out and hugged her gently around the waist. "Hi, Mama."

"Oh." She jolted. "You scared me." She dipped her head to the side and kissed Claire's forehead. She then cupped her palm around her daughter's chin. "Hungry?"

Belinda sidled next to them. "Starved."

Mama rustled the top of her hair. "Good."

As bad as her day had been at school with the Lavender Girls, it no longer mattered. Mama's face was no longer pasty white but instead emitted a warm glow. Her motherly kiss still tingled on her skin. Donuts topped off the kiss and the glow.

Was this what it felt like to count her blessings?

Mama pointed with her paring knife and told them the same thing she probably told the boys. "Neecy made donuts. Help yourselves to one and a glass of milk."

Lolly skipped into the kitchen from the backyard. "The boys don't let me play kick the can."

Claire corrected her sister's word choice. "It's won't, Lolly, not don't." She turned to scold her brothers but they were no longer at the table. She nudged Belinda. "Those boys gobbled their treats like wolves."

They giggled as each took a donut and moved to the table. After Belinda sat, Claire went to the refrigerator. "I'll get the milk."

"Thank ya." She bit into her cinnamon-sugar donut twist.

She laughed at her friend's yum-yums through a mouth full of the pastry.

Lolly stayed next to Mama with the tip of her finger in her mouth. "Can I sit with you girls?"

She pulled the pitcher of milk from the refrigerator. "Since when do you call us girls?"

"Don't know."

"Sometimes you sound too old for your age." After she filled their glasses with milk, she bit into the delicious donut, chewed, and allowed the flavors to melt on her tongue. She swallowed. "So. Did you have fun here today with Grandma Neecy?"

Wrapping her arms around herself, Lolly beamed. "Yeah, Sissy Pie. And I helped her with the donuts." She ran to where the donuts were lined up on a towel on the counter to cool. "See?" She aimed her tiny finger. "These ones are mine."

Claire stood to inspect them. Her sister's donuts were shaped more like a hot dog instead of a twist. "Good job. Now, see, this proves you are getting so big. Save me one of yours for after supper."

Lolly bunched her skirt in her two hands and swayed and hummed. Out of the corner of her eye, Claire noticed as her sister grabbed a funny-shaped donut and stuck it in her pocket. "For me for later?" Lolly grinned and nodded.

She swallowed the last of her milk but had some donut left. "Mama? Do we have enough milk for me to have another glass?"

"Help yourself." She waved toward the refrigerator. "With Bossy here, we have all we need and then some. Drink up because we may have to buy another refrigerator just to hold Goat and Bossy milk." She chuckled. "Imagine. We're so blessed because of you, Neecy."

Claire stopped mid-step in front of the refrigerator. *Mama laughed.*

Grandma Neecy wiped her hands on her apron. "Ya, know, it's my pleasure and really, I'm so grateful." She tossed her braids over her shoulders. "I was too sad when y'all left. Felt like I'd lost part of my family."

Mama hugged the older woman in a one arm hug— then whispered in her friend's ear. As she lifted the milk jug she did not know what was said, but both women giggled.

It was so good to see her mother happy. *Thank you, Lord, for the blessings.* Her prayer startled her. Yes, she could count her blessings, even on a bad day.

Liam hollered, "We want more donuts."

"Yeah." Grayson came in behind him.

Mama glanced over her shoulder at them. "Where are your manners? You forgot the 'please' with your request. And no. You'll spoil your appetite. But you may have more milk."

They scrambled to refill their glasses. Liam reached for the cow milk. "I want this kind."

Grayson grabbed the goat milk. "This is better."

Belinda licked her mouth and then her fingers. "How ya boys likin' school?"

Grayson poured himself a glass and then took a slurp before he responded. "Good." He turned to Liam. "Do I have a milk mustache?"

Liam frowned at him and faced Belinda. "Yeah, school is fun. I like being with my buddies again."

"You'll never guess who's at my school." She had to tell Liam what was going on.

He set down his half empty glass. "I give up."

"No. Guess."

"Give me a hint."

Belinda winked at Claire. "Two girls in our grade from Gallagher Springs and they're bullies."

The glass of milk in his hand hovered in midair. "No sir." He looked from one to the other as if watching a humming bird flit in the air. "Those Lavender Girls?"

"Yep." Belinda swatted at a fly.

His eyes narrowed. "Whatcha' going to do, Claire?"

"We've already had problems with them, so I don't know."

"But." Belinda chimed in. "We've started our own group with me, Claire, and Lizbeth." She flicked a crumb off the table with her finger. "We're not sure what to call ourselves."

Grayson raised his hand as though he was in class. "I know, I know."

Everyone grew silent.

"How about the Better Girls Club?"

"We could use those initials." Claire drummed her fingers on the table. "The BG Club."

"I like it." Belinda slapped the table.

"Me too," Liam said.

Grayson puffed out his chest. "It was my idea."

With her finger, Belinda corralled more crumbs in a tiny heap on the table. "But will Lizbeth like it?"

"We can only hope."

Next morning, after the girls told Lizbeth the name suggested for their club. Lizbeth beamed. "I love it. BG Club. It sounds sophisticated. Don't you think?"

The other two girls nodded.

As Claire listened to her friends chatter on about what they would do in the club, she realized something. Even though she'd known Lizbeth longer, she cared more for Belinda. Why was that? Was it because they had been tossed into a difficult time back in Gallagher Springs? Seemed like she and Lizbeth never had anything serious throw them together.

So a long-time, easy-going friendship may not mean as much as a few months of ups and downs with a new friendship? If so, then did it mean it's not the amount of time you spent with a friend that counts—instead it's the difficulties a girl goes through with a new friend, which draws them closer than years could with another friend?

With an inward shrug, Claire shook off the deep thoughts—sure that she was a traitor to Lizbeth.

Right then and there, she vowed not to show favoritism between her two best friends. In her opinion, to pick a favorite would be the ultimate mean act.

~^~^~

Mama slipped a letter under Claire's dinner plate. Most everyone had finished and left the table. She cleared her throat. "You might want to read that."

She retrieved the letter, opened the tri-folded sheet of paper, and read out loud.

"Dear Dotty, Pete, and children,

"I hope this letter finds you settled and doing well back home in Oregon. We are having the time of our lives here in Alaska. Dotty, your dad fishes every day while I hike the easier trails near our cabin in the woods.

"We love Alaska. We have decided to stay until the threat of heavy snows. Your dad is trying to convince me to live here through the winter, but I would miss you, Pete, and the children.

"This is not a newsy letter because we have a request. Mother is becoming too lonely by herself in Wonder Pass. I found this out when she wrote to me. Would you and Pete take her in for a few months until we return? I would so appreciate this. Mother would love spending time with you and the children."

With those words, Claire's heart sank. She stared at Mama. "But, Grandmother Walker is grumpy. I don't think she gets along with anyone." She slapped her hand over her mouth. "I'm sorry."

Daddy scooted back his chair and stood beside Mama. "Finish the letter."

"So if it's not a problem, please get in contact with Mother and arrange a time to pick her up.

"Thank you. We love each of you."

Claire slumped in her chair and sensed the stare of too many eyeballs. Daddy touched the top of her head. "For sure, I'll need to finish the apartment for Grandmother Walker." He moved his hand from Claire. "It should take about a month." Daddy called the boys in from the kitchen where they had started the cleanup. "Boys, come here. We'll need to work on the apartment this weekend. Grandmother Walker is coming to live with us for awhile."

Liam worried his thumb and index finger together. "I like helping you build ... but, Daddy, she's a mean old lady."

"She's not nice like Grandma Neecy." Grayson leaned into Daddy's side.

Claire squirmed in her chair. "She's also going to need help which means more work for us." She stood and pushed her chair under the table and waited for him to agree.

"Now Claire." Mama spoke before he could. "I'd like my grandmother to come for a visit. It's not permanent. We'll all pull together and make her time comfortable."

Grandma Neecy stood at the dining room table. "I agree. We can't neglect the older folk. It's not fittin'." She placed her hands on her bulging waist, readjusted her dress belt, and studied the kids' faces. "Besides, the more the merrier I always say."

Claire muttered. "Not in this case."

"What's that ya say?"

"Nothing." She grabbed a couple of dirty plates and dragged her feet toward the kitchen where Belinda was putting away the leftover food.

Before bedtime, she caught Daddy alone at the sink. "Daddy, what about a private place for Grandma Neecy and Belinda? They may be staying with us a long while."

He scrubbed his fingers through his red, curly beard. "I've thought about this and have already put an idea into motion." He yawned, moisture gleaming in his eyes as always when he yawned. "My buddy over in Wonder Pass has a boxcar."

Claire squinted. "What's that?"

"I said it wrong." He wiped at his face. "It's actually the caboose of a train. He remodeled it for his wife's mother.

She planned to live in it on their property, but she died a month ago."

She never knew what to think or even say when she heard a person was no longer alive. She'd never known anyone she cared about who was there one day and then they weren't. "I've never seen the inside of a caboose."

"Well, you're about to." Daddy grinned. "Buster is willing to sell it to me. He's allowing me to make payments because of our circumstances. You know, with an overflow of people so quickly." He winked. "How's that for fast action?"

Her mouth formed an O. "How soon can we get it?"

"Tomorrow, and I've already cleared it with Neecy. She's excited to live in a caboose, and that allows us to get Grandmother Walker on Sunday."

"Oh." She didn't dare ask where her great-grandmother would sleep.

Daddy yawned even louder. "Tomorrow will be a busy day. You'll keep the little kids inside after the caboose arrives and until the truck that hauls it leaves."

"Sure, Daddy." She found it hard to believe. A caboose for a home. And on their property. She couldn't wait to discuss this with Belinda in the morning and her girlfriends on Monday.

And she'd give her tired brain a rest from thinking about her great-grandmother whose middle name should be Cranky.

11

Daddy shook Claire's shoulder before the sun was shining through her windows. In turn, she woke Grandma Neecy and Belinda. The three of them became busy cooking mouth-watering biscuits, sausage gravy, and bacon.

Her father had made his cowboy coffee. The smell drove her to take a humongous whiff, even though she didn't like the taste. Grandma Neecy yawned. "Bless yer dear Daddy's heart." She poured a splash of milk into her coffee cup and topped off Belinda's extended cup.

Claire cast a glance at the two of them while she continued to mix flour, baking powder, and salt in an extra large mixing bowl. "How can you two stand that bitter drink?"

Belinda stood next to her friend and slurped her coffee and smacked her lips. "Ahhh. Nice and warm." She nudged Claire's arm. "Go on. Try it. I made yours with lots of milk and a little coffee. Just right for you, little buddy." She tapped the side of the cup at Claire's elbow. "See? It's the color of a newborn fawn's spots, where ours is as tan as a cougar." She nudged her again. "Go ahead. Or are you chicken?"

She glared at the coffee. She hated the stuff. But her parents always drank it coal black. Maybe. She creased her nose. Maybe not.

"You can't knock it until ya try it." She blinked a couple of times and stretched her long arms over her head. "See? Now I'm awake."

Okay. Well. She took hold of the slender handle of what was really a teacup and sniffed. Why did it have to smell so good? She could take one sip and declare it was not for her. Get Belinda off her back.

She wiggled her fingers at Claire as in "drink your coffee."

Claire twisted the cup half a turn to avoid the chip, sipped, and—savored, enjoyed, memorized the hot brew on her tongue. She swallowed. "This is delicious." She chuckled and returned to her biscuit makings.

She still marveled over the happy flavor of her coffee when Belinda interrupted her thoughts.

"Can ya believe it? We getta live in a caboose." She leaned her elbows on the counter, her coffee cup between her hands.

She gave the dry ingredients another swirl with her wooden spoon and took another sip of coffee. "Yeah, I'm excited for you two." After she dumped a couple of large spoonfuls of lard into the bowl, she mixed it into the flour.

Belinda pulled the cast iron skillet from the woodstove's warming shelf above the stove. "Yes, siree, we are caboosers."

Her mouth twitched at her friend's choice of words. Behind her, Grandma Neecy made it clear that she enjoyed

Daddy's special coffee. She *ahh*ed after each swallow.
"Girls," the older woman began, "I've never been inside a
caboose. It'll be a wonder for sure to live in one, don't ya
know."

Claire glanced at Belinda. "Maybe I can spend the
night sometimes. Won't that be fun?"

"Yeppers."

She took another drink of the lukewarm coffee. It
made her feel grownup. As she mixed the lard until the
dough was little pea-sized balls, a realization smacked her
upside the head. "Hey." She stopped mixing.

Belinda worked at making gravy on the wood
cookstove. "Hey, what?"

"Excuse me, darlin'. I need to set the table." Claire
ducked her head so Grandma Neecy could gather plates from
the cabinet.

When Grandma moved away, she faced Belinda.
"Your birthday is coming up."

"Sure enough." She stopped stirring the gravy. "I'll
be a teenager."

As Grandma Neecy opened the utensil drawer, she
gasped. "Deliver me." Her face paled, and she continued to
count the forks needed for breakfast.

When Grandma Neecy placed the plates and forks on
the table, she hurried from the kitchen. Claire moved over to
the stove and whispered, "Is something wrong?"

She craned her neck where her grandma had
disappeared into the living room. She turned back to stir the
gravy again. One corner of her mouth lifted in a smile. "I
think she just figured out I'm no longer a little girl."

"Ohhh." She went back to the counter where she added warm milk to the almost finished biscuit makings. She drank the last of her coffee and kneaded the dough. "Mama got teary-eyed when we celebrated my thirteenth birthday last year."

"Really?"

"Mama even gave me a tall grownup-looking doll. I remember blinking at the doll, stunned speechless." She washed the lard and flour off her hands and dried them. "I think she was ready for my reaction because she said, 'This is your last doll. You are now too old for them.'"

Grandma Neecy hurried back in and started frying bacon. Her face flushed and eyes shimmering.

Belinda didn't respond. Claire was certain they couldn't discuss thirteenth birthdays with Grandma Neecy in the room.

Moments later, Daddy rushed in and poured a cup of coffee. "Claire. Make more coffee, please. Buster's here." He hurried from the kitchen and left by the front door.

"I've never made coffee before."

"I'll do it." Grandma Neecy left the bacon to fry. "Belinda, take over at the stove."

As she kneaded the dough, she hoped, hoped, hoped setting up the caboose went smoothly for Daddy. On second thought, she prayed it so.

~∧~∧~

On Claire's silent amen, the truck and trailer that hauled the caboose rumbled into the circle driveway.

The girls, along with Grandma Neecy, watched the caboose sway by the window while they stood in the safety of the living room.

Grandma Neecy sighed. "I'm too excited. Yer daddy told me last night they'd place the caboose next to the outside fence of the backyard."

"Cause ya know, Claire, if the bathroom's busy inside the house, we've got the outhouse a few steps away." Belinda stuck out her tongue between her teeth and giggled.

"Makes perfect sense." She headed toward the kitchen to finish shaping the biscuits.

Belinda followed close behind. "I'm famished."

She halted her steps, and her friend bumped against her with a whump. "What did you just say?"

Her eyes grew as round as dinner plates. "Uhhh, I'm famished …"

"Who taught you the word famish? Did you read it in a book? Was it a teacher?" She couldn't help but grin.

"I don't know. It just—popped into my head."

"Belinda Cruz, you are a wonder." She entered the kitchen, and they both got back to baking and cooking.

The patter of feet came into the kitchen with Grandma Neecy. "The boys are awake and dressed and will be down soon." Feather yawned where he nestled in her arms. His head wobbled as though his sleep got interrupted. Lolly clutched Grandma's apron with one hand and rubbed her eyes with the other. "Let's get this little fella some milk." She placed the baby in his highchair. "That'll wake him."

When she placed the cup in front of him, Feather dove for it. "My." He gulped the milk, some dribbled down his chin. Claire grinned. He would be one-year-old soon. Had it been almost a year since Daddy rushed Mama and Feather to the hospital after the home birth? Her grin slipped and her teeth clenched.

Her brothers shuffled into the kitchen as Mama hobbled on her crutches behind them. "Should we wait for Daddy or eat without him?"

"We'll eat without him, Claire." Mama passed by her and reached for a coffee cup. "We can keep his and Buster's food in the warmer."

"Here, Mama, let me fill your cup." She took it from her. "You go sit down. I had my first cup of coffee with a lot of milk."

"Oh? You enjoyed it?"

"Yes, Mama."

"Good morning, Neecy and children," Mama said, and everyone returned the greeting.

Right as Grandma Neecy placed the bowl of golden-crusted biscuits at the center of the table, Mama took her seat. Belinda set the platter of eggs on one side of the biscuits and the plate of bacon on the other side.

Liam popped up from his chair and helped Mama scoot closer to the table. "Thank you, Son." He patted her shoulder and sat back down. "Once everyone is seated, would you ask the blessing?"

"Yes, Mama."

Once all were seated, Mama motioned to Liam. He bowed his head, and they all did likewise. "Dear Lord, thank you for this food and thank you for the people who cooked it. In Jesus' name. Amen."

And everyone said amen.

"When we gonna see the coose?"

"It's called a caboose, Lolly." Claire touched her arm. "And don't talk with your mouth full."

"Okay." She covered her mouth, chewed, and then swallowed. "Sorry, Sissy Pie." She glanced at Mama. "We gonna ride it like a train, Mama?"

The boys snickered, Belinda choked on her drink, and Claire's jaw hardened to manage a straight expression.

"Course not, silly." Liam wiped his mouth with a napkin. "It's part of *a* train, not *the* train."

"Oh, I see."

"No, you don't." Grayson giggled.

"I do so." Her bottom lip ballooned into a pout.

The older girls exchanged glances and Claire said, "Just eat." But Lolly didn't listen.

"Grandma Neecy, do you wanna live in a train?"

"Sure do." She dabbed at her mouth. "It'll be interestin', don't ya know."

Lolly spooned another mouthful of eggs and watched Grandma Neecy the whole time she ate. "May I sleep at your train some day?"

Grayson giggle-snorted.

"It's not funny."

"Yeah, you keep calling the caboose a train."

"Mama, make him stop."

A gleam appeared in Mama's eyes as she chewed on a piece of bacon. After she swallowed, she placed her hands on the table. "Now, Grayson."

"I can't help it. She says the funniest things."

"I do not." She stood and pushed her chair back with a squeak.

Claire whispered in her sister's ear, "Honey, you need to calm down. You know Grayson gets the giggles real easy."

Mama buttered another biscuit. "Son, she doesn't understand your kind of humor."

"Oh, alright." He scooped a spoonful of gravy into his mouth.

"She's too touchy." Liam stuffed more food in and chewed.

"Am not."

Claire settled back into her chair. "Eat."

Moments later, Belinda lifted her empty plate. "I'll start the dishwater."

Everyone helped clean the table, while Grandma Neecy prepared a plate for Daddy and one for Buster and set them on the warming shelves of the cookstove. Mama stayed at the table and sipped another cup of coffee and played patty cake with the baby.

His giggles chased circles around the warm room.

As Feather took a breath from the last round of laughter, someone knocked on the front door. Liam rushed over to answer it. "What are you doing here?"

The person murmured a reply.

Claire's heart plummeted.

Surely not.

12

Claire froze. Her hands stilled while washing a dish. How did they find where she lived?

Belinda filled the sink with rinse water as Claire lowered her voice. "I wonder who's here." Although, she knew and she would not allow it. They had no right to invade their home.

Belinda shrugged. "Go see."

"I think it's them."

"What?" She furrowed her one brow. "Who?"

"Never mind." She left and slowed by Mama where she sat nearest the entryway to the living room. She touched the top metal rail on the back of her chair. More voices from the visitors.

Her hand fell to her side. She had to meet them, so she walked through the entryway and to the front door. Liam glared at her. "Why did you give them our address?"

She pursed her lips. The Lavender Girls stepped inside, and their eyes roamed the room. As she moved past Liam, she hissed, "Shush, I didn't."

She motioned Wendy and Kaye to step back out the door. Her brother followed so close his breath rustled the stray hairs on her neck. She reached behind her and nudged him away. When she shut the door, Laddie licked her other hand.

A delicate sniffle escaped from Wendy. "Nice old house you have here, ClaireLee." Her lips twitched.

It was a challenge. Only a challenge. And she never could back down from one. "Remember, Wendy? It's just Claire."

Kaye waved her hands in defense. "Slight mistake. You'll remember next time, right Wendy?"

"Of course."

With a hand on her hip, Claire wanted to ask questions. Questions she knew they expected. Why are you here? How did you find me?

"I can't invite you in. I've got a ton of work today." Claire glanced at the shiny black car in the driveway and recognized Kaye's dad in the driver's seat. The two uninvited guests creased their foreheads as though in disbelief as she took a backward step. "See you at school on Monday." She hurried inside, tugged Laddie's collar to join her, and then shut the door.

If Claire could help it, no way would Mama know who had been at the door. What if she recognized Kaye? Would Mama even remember though? Probably not, but she locked the front door for good measure.

As she moved away, Belinda met her. "You're as pale as a frog's belly. Who was it?" She patted Laddie's head.

She motioned for her friend to hush and led her past Mama and Feather still playing at the table. At the sink, dishes still waited. Belinda drew out a cup from the rinse water and let the excess water drain. "Spit it out."

"The Lavender Girls."

The dish in Belinda's fingers slipped back into the water. "Ya gotta be kiddin'."

She scrubbed on a plate. Extra hard. "No. Wish I were." She handed the plate to Belinda. When her friend didn't say anymore, she figured she'd been struck speechless.

Long minutes passed while Belinda shifted her feet. "Did they say what they wanted?"

"To bug us? Check out where we live? Maybe they're bored. Harassing us would keep those two entertained." She handed Belinda a glass. "All I know is . . . I got rid of them."

"Do ya think your ma noticed?"

They both glanced at her still at play with Feather. "No." She grabbed a greasy skillet and scrubbed. She had to erase those bullies from her mind. "Daddy must be getting hungry."

Belinda poked her with a finger. "They've got to eat, and I wanna see that ol' caboose."

After they finished the dishes, the two friends each took a full plate in one hand and a cup of coffee in the other, then headed to the back porch. A loud thump sounded from the direction Daddy and Buster were setting up the caboose. An explosion of Portuguese words flew through the air.

Uh-oh.

~∧~∧~

The kids never bothered to shut the back porch door all the way on their way out or in. Glad about that for once, Claire bumped it open and took two steps into the backyard. She gasped. Behind her, Belinda mumbled. "I'll be a monkey's uncle."

The red caboose towered over the cedar fence.

The girls hurried through the open gate. "Looky at them yellow stripes along the sides below the windows. It looks like a circus caboose."

"Oh, no. Daddy has it on blocks, and one side of the caboose fell off."

"I don't think yer daddy's gonna want to eat right now."

The two men came around to the side of the caboose where it fell. Her father knelt and examined the area and glanced up. "I see food and drink coming our way, Buster. Ready for a break?"

"Sounds like a winner, Pete."

"Just in time, girls. You read our minds."

"What do we have here?" Buster said. "Service and with a smile."

"Are you having problems, Daddy?" The girls handed them their plates. The men said thank you and sat on a long wooden bench within the fenced yard.

He sipped his coffee. "Yep, we are, but we'll get it fixed."

Buster chewed on a thick slice of bacon. "It's nothing we can't handle. We'll jack it up again and make sure the wheel is centered better over on the block." He paused for a slurp of coffee. "Once that's done, your company can move right in." He took another bite of bacon and watched the girls. "How many are living in it?"

"Me and my grandma."

"Good." He raised his cup. "Plenty of room for two. More than that and it gets too cozy."

After the men ate and got the wheel of the caboose settled on a solid block, Buster led them on a tour of the inside.

"This could be my grandma's bed, and this one here could be mine."

Claire's eyes roved over the snug and remodeled caboose. Windows dressed with frilly, light blue curtains with white polka-dots lined the long walls. Beneath the windows, the wainscoting had a shiny coat on the wood. In the middle of the caboose, her vision took in a tiny sitting area with a sofa and chair. After that, a table and two chairs stood ready for Belinda and Grandma Neecy to eat their meals.

A miniature wood burning stove sat between the table and the kitchen, ready to provide heat in winter.

Next, the kitchen area used both sides of the aisle. A sink, counter space, and cupboards were on one side. Across from it sat a tiny stovetop, oven, and refrigerator. Belinda opened the refrigerator and the girls peeked inside—a small-scale freezer was on top.

At the caboose's second entry, Belinda opened two closet doors across from each other. "Looks like you can open these only when the caboose door is shut." She peered inside the compact spaces. There was a place to hang clothes above and two drawers below.

As she shut one closet door, Claire tried the caboose door, but it wouldn't budge.

Buster came near. "You're going to want to keep that door locked. It will give you more room and in cold weather it'll keep the heat in much better."

As the little group left the caboose, the girls said goodbye to Buster. They almost bumped into Grandma Neecy at the backyard gate. Her arms were weighed down with a gallon jar of Bossy's milk and a quart jar of Goat's milk. "Is the caboose cute, Belinda?"

"You're going to really like it, Grandma."

The girls offered to carry the milk, and Grandma Neecy led the way. "We're going to separate the cream from last night's milk so we can make more butter."

On the walk to the house and once inside, Belinda told her grandma how homey and colorful the interior was in their new living quarters. Grandma Neecy grinned. "When we're done, y'all have to show me around."

After the girls made the butter, they watched Grandma Neecy make the cheese from the goat milk. When the cheese was in the cloth and hung to drain, Claire's thoughts made a U-turn. An unwanted visitor would arrive tomorrow.

The old woman always got on her last nerve.

~^~^~

Grandmother Walker knew how to do two things. How to complain and how to rearrange the family's routine like a hair-pin curve down a mountain.

"But, Daddy, why do I have to give her my room? Let *her* take the sofa." She packed his lunch for work as they both talked. Grandmother Walker informed him she would not be ready to come to their house on Sunday. When she was ready, she'd let them know.

And Claire was already unhappy about the way Monday started with the news she'd have to give her entire room to Grandmother Walker. Sure as the world turned, she would boss around the whole family. Even Grandma Neecy.

"Done with my lunch pail, Claire?"

She snapped shut the lid. "Please don't give her my room."

He lifted the pail off the counter and lingered next to her. "Listen, ClaireBear, this can't be helped. I don't really want her here anymore than you do."

"You're doing this for Mama then?"

He clamped a hand on her shoulder and she looked up at him. "Chin up. Grandmother Walker will visit for a few weeks. She'll get so tired of the noise the kids make, she'll be glad to return to her quiet cottage on Rouge River."

"But Nana expects us to keep her maybe even all winter." She smoothed strands of hair from her face. "I'll be miserable."

"I'll see if Neecy will eventually share her caboose with you." He dipped his jaw. "How does that sound?"

"But you said you'd get the apartment finished for Grandmother Walker."

He glanced at the wall clock. "I know I did but now I've got to make payments on the caboose. They aren't cheap. I'll have no leftover cash to finish the apartment."

"Oh, okay. I didn't think of that." She folded her hands as if she was about to pray. "Please. Let's at least set a time for when I might stay in the caboose. How about two weeks after she gets here?"

He chuckled. "You drive a hard bargain, daughter." He kissed the top of her head, with an "Okay", and clomped from the house.

I love my daddy.

As the quiet of the kitchen surrounded her, she glanced at the clock. 6:00 a.m. Almost time to wake the boys up for school. Grandma Neecy and Belinda would be coming through the back porch door any second, so they could use the indoor bathroom before the boys needed it. And sure enough, the porch door opened and shut.

She went into the boys' room to wake them. She shook Liam awake and then Grayson. "Time for school."

"I hate Mondays." Liam crawled off the bed and yawned. "Weekends are never long enough during school."

She rolled her eyes and left the room before his grumpy mood took aim at her. Why did some people have to grouch at others in the mornings? She'd never understand.

That left her with the thought of facing the Lavender Girls today. After she'd told them they had to leave because she was too busy to visit.

Claire was in for it now, and she scowled. They would give her no peace.

13

The two friends raised their voices above the other students on the bus. They were making birthday party plans for Belinda. Claire bent closer to her so she would no longer strain her vocal chords. "We'll invite the girls I think will come." She counted them by name on her fingers.

She stopped at ten, and Belinda smiled. "Ten's a good size group. Now let's figure out the dessert. I could see if Grandma will bake chocolate cupcakes instead of a cake."

"Cupcakes?" She tilted her head. "Mama always makes those. Instead, we'll make an oblong cake."

"Let's do both. With only twelve of us girls, we'll have enough for leftovers."

Claire soft-punched her friend's arm. "Leave it to you to plan enough food so there's seconds."

"Speaking of food, let's roast hotdogs and have real hotdog buns. Not bread slices. What do ya say?"

"Sure. We'll roast marshmallows too."

She clapped her palms on her thighs and let out a loud *yahoo*. "This'll be the best birthday."

"Thirteen is a big deal." She stood, smoothed the back of her skirt, and sat. "It should be the best." She paused.

"Is your grandma happy here? Maybe especially now that she has her own funny little house?"

"Oh, yeah, she's lovin' it here. She told me last night that with my mama gone to Hollywood and my uncles married with families and moved to yonder states, she was ready for a change. She told me she was gettin' heart sick." She leaned back into her seat. "Sad, huh?"

Poor Grandma Neecy. "Yes, very sad. But you're here now." She slipped her arm through her friend's.

As the driver turned into the junior high parking lot, a gust of wind rocked the bus. Was this a sign of an early winter?

Claire hoped not. An indoor birthday party was never as much fun as an outdoor one.

~^~^~

Since the birthday party was planned for the upcoming Saturday, she introduced Belinda to the girls invited. A verbal invite came with introductions and each girl accepted. She assured them there would be no need for presents since it was late notice. But before she could announce no gifts, Lorene Klaas had walked off.

After lunch, the BGs were in the restroom where they washed their hands and chatted at the semi-circular wash fountain sink. The Lavenders Girls' entry was reflected in mirror. "We hear you are putting on a birthday party Saturday."

No one spoke until Belinda angled her head, still facing the mirror. "Yep." She continued to soap up her hands.

Claire moved to lean against the wall closer to the door. It made no sense to tell them they weren't invited. They should know that.

"So." Kaye began. "What time does the party start?"

Lizbeth gasped. She shook her hands over the sink and glanced up at the bullies as they stood near the paper towel dispenser.

Belinda's shoe lifted from the sink's foot control. The water shut off. Like Lizbeth, she waved her hands to get rid of excess water. She turned, reached around the bullies for a paper towel, and dried her hands. She cocked her one good brow. "What's it to ya?" She nodded at Lizbeth and Claire and they followed her as she shoved the door open with her broad shoulder.

Claire whispered. "They're so bold."

"No surprise." Belinda walked faster. "They disgust me."

Lizbeth sputtered her words. "I, I never, in all my life met such, such rude girls."

"You're going too fast." Claire stumbled. "Are your feet also angry?"

"Nah." She slowed when they came near the large pine tree at the edge of the school yard. She leaned against the tree and placed the bottom of her shoe on the trunk. "I guess I didn't see that one coming. Mad at myself for it, more than anythin'."

Claire nabbed a pine cone off the ground. "It did cross my mind, but I thought even they wouldn't stoop so low." She released a breath. "This is going to be a long, long school year, girls."

Lizbeth fiddled with the top button of her blouse. "Do you think they knew we wouldn't invite them? Maybe we should."

The other two girls stared at her. "No."

Mary Hammer strolled over to them. "Hi."

"Hi." Claire flicked a pine nut to the ground. "We're glad you plan to attend Belinda's birthday party."

"I wouldn't miss it. But that's not why I came over here." Mary leaned against the tree. "You know those new girls?"

"Do we ever." Belinda snorted.

"Well, they heard some of us talking about being invited to your party on Saturday ..." She blinked and paused as though figuring out what to say next. "Kaye told me they didn't know anything about a party, and asked me why they weren't invited. Then, Wendy said, 'It's rude to not invite us just because we're new students.'"

"Wait, wait, wait." Belinda waved both hands over her head. "Believe me, that isn't why."

"Oh."

The bell rang and drowned out her next words. Claire nudged her. "We better go."

Mary kept pace with them. "I don't mean to gossip, but where did they come from? They seem, I don't know ... out of place."

"That's just it." Claire spread her hands as they approached the steps of the school. "They're from a big city, and I'm not sure why that would matter but it seems to with these girls."

There was no more time to explain—they had to get to choir practice. And with only a few empty seats left, the girls had to split up. Claire sat next to Lorene Klaas. "Hi Lorene."

The edges of her mouth lifted in a tiny smile, but she kept her lips pursed. Claire squirmed. She never knew what to do when someone didn't return a verbal greeting. Everyone in school knew she was quiet. An A student, she had nothing to prove. Besides, her dad owned the largest mill in their little valley. The Klaas Lumber Mill.

She picked at a jagged nail on her index finger but stopped her nervous habit when interrupted by a *swoosh* of air behind her. Whoever it was, they almost touched her. She glanced over her shoulder. Kaye sat one seat behind. Oh, bother. To keep her mind off the trouble sure to come, she studied who was in class today.

Someone tapped her shoulder. "About your party," Kaye said.

"What about it?" Intimidated, but she refused to look at her. And she longed for the choir teacher to come into the room.

"It's like this, ClaireLee." She paused. "We are always invited to parties."

Kaye was attempting to anger her, and she would not fall for it. Not again.

At that moment, Mr. Konklin appeared in the doorway. His fancy shoes clicked on the linoleum and sounded like a tap dancer. His tenor voice, chipper as always, began to sing their warm ups. "Me, me, me." Everyone echoed him.

He continued to sing, waving the students to stand. He went up another note. "Me, me, me." After a few more me, me, me's, Mr. Konklin swung his hand in the air. He made a fist as a signal for them to cut off at the last note. In a dramatic wave of both hands, he coached everyone to sit.

"He's no orchestra conductor." Wendy's voice boomed loud and clear. "Who's he trying to impress?"

Mr. Konklin's gaze roamed, and then settled on Wendy. She sat on the first row near the door. Claire held her breath. He had a reputation to never show anger, but she'd heard about his no-nonsense method for disruptive students. He waved his hand toward the door as in, *you may leave.* "Your point, Miss Lavender?" His smile froze like a mask.

She raised her chin and sniffed and stared right back at him.

Mr. Konklin let his hand fall to his side. "I thought as much." He sat down on the piano bench. "We're going to practice age-old Christmas songs for our performance in early December. Miss Klaas, will you pass around the sheet music?" He nodded toward a pile of sheet music on the music stand he often stood behind and began to play the notes to a very familiar carol. "Class, 'Silent Night' was composed in 1818 by Franz Xaver Gruber. Joseph Mohr wrote the lyrics."

After each student had their copy, Mr. Konklin played a few more stanzas. He then moved students around after he listened to their voices. Claire was paired with Wendy, both being high soprano. Lizbeth and Kaye were second sopranos. Belinda and Lorene were altos. Claire scooted over a bit from the bully. Being next to her made her knees as weak as a newborn calf.

They practiced "Silent Night" a few times before the school bell rang to end class. Students waited until Mr. Konklin said they could leave. Once dismissed, they rushed to the door. Everyone knew the time to get to another class was a matter of five minutes.

Claire fell into step next to Lorene. "If you come to the birthday party, there's no need to bring presents."

"Okay. I'll be there."

Someone behind them said, "We'll not take *no* for an answer, Claire."

She continued to keep in pace with Lorene. She really didn't want trouble because she was now afraid of her own temper.

"Invited or not, we *will* be at your party." Wendy sashayed past the two girls with Kaye following.

Lorene stopped and muttered.

"Did you say something?" She took two backward steps to Lorene's side.

She crossed her arms. "What was that all about, and who is she? Who's her friend?"

"It would take too much time to explain."

Lorene began walking again. "You obviously know them from somewhere."

"Belinda and I went to school with them last year in California."

Moving toward science class, they stopped at the open door. "You were the talk of the first week of school last year when you didn't show for sixth grade. But now I understand." She smiled ever so slight.

"You have braces?"

"I do, but I don't advertize it."

Late bell rang, and the girls whisked into the room and to their seats. Now Claire understood why Lorene kept her mouth shut tight more than ever before.

~^~^~

Claire walked to her last class which also doubled as her homeroom and past Wendy and Kaye. Her stomach tightened with dread. She was supposed to recite a poem in front of the class. One she had chosen from a book of poems Mrs. Byers kept on a back shelf.

After everyone settled into their seats, the teacher called first one student and then another to recite poems. Too soon it was Claire's turn. She clenched her hands together.

As she stood before the class, a problem smacked her in the face. It wasn't that she didn't know her poem by heart—she did. The verses called to her the first time she read them and she would memorize this one and no other.

The trouble was the topic.

Heat crawled up her neck and smeared her face. Claire opened her mouth. She did what Mrs. Byers had instructed the class and to help them not forget lines, stutter over their poem, or freeze like she was doing right then.

She stared above the students' heads.

14

"My poem is by Elizabeth Barrett Browning and is titled, "How Do I Love Thee? Let Me Count the Ways."

Claire swallowed, shut her eyes, took a deep breath, and began.

"I love thee to the depth and breadth and height
My soul can reach, when feeling out of sight
For the ends of Being and ideal Grace.
I love thee to the level of every day's
Most quiet need, by sun and candle-light.
I love thee freely, as men strive for Right;
I love thee purely, as they turn from Praise.
I love thee with the passion put to use
In my old griefs, and with my childhood's faith.
I love thee with a love I seemed to lose
With my lost saints – I love thee with the breath,
Smiles, tears, of all my life! – and, if God choose,
I shall but love thee better after death."

Claire pursed her lips and peeked through one opened eye. Her chest clutched like a fist as she gazed at the faces. Most of the boys' eyes grew soft. Dreamy.

Their reaction startled her but then Mrs. Byers and the whole class clapped. When she sat down, she kept her gaze on the teacher. She was smiling. "Well done. You did not miss a word, nor did your voice falter."

She breathed out her relief that it was over ... not only that it was over, but that Mrs. Byers was pleased. Still, she decided she'd never read a sappy love poem in class ever again. She wanted to pinch herself for her blunder. What was she thinking to recite an intimate topic like love in front of a bunch of boys?

Just thinking of what she'd done made her face hot as a sunburn.

Jimmy Hawks leaned back. "Good job."

She didn't dare look at him, but she managed a thank you. She released another long breath as the teacher told everyone to get out their workbooks.

"Psst." Was someone trying to get her attention? Across the aisle and one seat back. Kaye Tyner whispered just loud enough. "What are you Juliet? Where's Romeo?" she snickered.

She wanted to scream, "shut up." But she counted the books on one of the shelves instead. Calmly taking a breath, she pulled out her workbook, flipped to the lesson, and plotted her revenge.

When the bell rang, Wendy sauntered toward Claire. She stopped at her desk and tapped her long, bubble gum pink fingernails on the desktop. "Were you aware the poem you recited is a funeral poem?"

Claire's lips parted. No way.

"Really?" Kaye sidled next to her bully friend. "It's not a love poem?"

"It's a love poem about dead people."

Kaye swiveled to face the kids as they were leaving the room. "Did you all know? The poem Claire recited is used at funerals." She slapped her palms together and rubbed them as though she knew a bit of dirt on someone. And she did.

Boys glared at Kaye as they walked past. Girls shook their heads. Some whispered and pointed at Kaye.

Claire straightened as tall as her four foot eleven and three fourths height allowed.

Wendy shrugged. "Read a poem's words more carefully, Claire. Or at least think about them before you stand before the class and look like a clown."

She battled away her tears when she noticed Lorene shoved back through the line of kids as they left the room. She stopped at Claire's side. "Let's go. We'll miss the bus." She hooked her arm through Claire's and faced the bullies. "Excuse us."

They headed straight toward the Lavender Girls but when they didn't budge, Lorene narrowed her eyes. "In other words, move." She reached out a palm. Wendy broke away from Kaye and stood to the side.

The girls got to the bus with no more problems, and Claire thanked her. She spotted Belinda and rushed to sit beside her friend.

Belinda's face was a bit flushed, and her mouth opened before Claire settled next to her. "You'll never believe what happened, little buddy."

"I've got news for you, too, but you go first."

"Well, get this." She lowered her voice. "In my PE class, everyone was dressed down in their issued exercise suits. Except for Kaye, again. Miss Rose blew her whistle. Ya know she just loves that ol' whistle … and then yelled, 'Kaye Tyner.' Kaye pointed at herself, and Miss Rose nodded. I couldn't hear what she said, but Kaye said real loud, 'I'm not wearing a monkey suit.'"

She gasped. "She yelled at the nicest teacher in the school?"

"I know, huh. And the other girls say she's been giving one excuse after another for not wearing the suit. Ya should have seen *her* outfit. Before today she wore her regular clothes. But rumor has it Miss Rose is about to give her an F for the class."

"Well, she deserves an F." As if she were at a movie theater and needed a snack, Claire dug into her lunch bag and pulled out a leftover sandwich. "What was she wearing?"

Belinda snorted. "She was wearin' black leotards. That's what one of the girls called them, with a matching short skirt." She sliced the side of her hand across her upper thigh. "That teensy thing came up to here. I've never seen anything like it."

"That outfit she wore sounds familiar."

"What?"

"My aunt took ballet when she was younger. I think you are describing what she dressed in when she went to her lessons."

"Ya know, Miss Rose did say something like PE was not a ballet class."

Another bite of her leftover berry sandwich, and Claire purred at the yummy delight. The jam-soaked bread filled the tiny holes with fruity sweetness. She chewed and swallowed. "I remember when Auntie's skirt would fan like an umbrella when she twirled."

"Never heard of ballet before today."

"Did she get benched?"

"Yeah, that was after she told Miss Rose she'd never wear a monkey suit. Really, she's been benched ever since I've been here."

Finished with her sandwich, Claire wadded her sack. "Kaye Tyner *will* get an F in PE—"

"I don't think she cares." Belinda was shaking her head before Claire even finished her sentence. "I wonder if there's another reason she won't wear the suit."

"Maybe she's extra modest. Back in Gallagher Springs, I don't remember her undressing around us girls before or after swim class. Do you?"

"Now that ya mention it, no." Belinda snapped her fingers. "Ya know what else? She always wore dark tights with her swim suit. Didn't that seem strange?"

She agreed, and then changed the subject. She told Belinda every detail about her poem—how if she would have thought it through, she would have never recited that poem to a room full of boys. She was about to tell Belinda what Wendy said about the poem being a funeral poem, but she stopped herself. She didn't want to upset Belinda over another bully tactic from the Lavender Girls.

She figured Belinda had enough. Claire sure had her fill to overflowing.

~∧~∧~

The two friends were not bothered by the Lavender Girls for the next few days … except for the knowing looks the mean girls gave them. They acted as if they wanted to drive home the fact they'd be at the party, invited or not.

Claire spotted Lizbeth waiting near the bus lane at the junior high. She waved at them as they got off the bus. "Did you two miss me?"

"Well, sure." Belinda grinned back. "Were ya sick?"

"No, but my little brothers were sick with the flu. I helped my mother nurse them back to health." She bent closer. "Thank goodness, Mother didn't expect me to clean the vomit. That was her job. But I did have to bathe them afterward."

Before Claire had a chance to speak, Belinda blurted. "We think Kaye has a secret."

"Why do you say that?"

She told Lizbeth what happened in PE with Miss Rose. She didn't say much, just listened as they headed to the entry of the school hallway. Wendy and Kaye stood at the entrance, hands on hips. "We're coming to your party, Claire."

"Why won't ya wear the gym suit, Kaye?"

"None of your business." She stood stone still, her snooty expression a mask.

"It is so, if I have to wear one and the whole class has to wear one. So that's not an excuse."

Claire touched Belinda's arm. "Let's go."

Wendy moved closer. "Like Kaye said, we're coming to your party."

"Don't, waste your dad's gas. We did not invite ya."

"What's this about not inviting new students to a birthday party?" Miss Rose, the very tall and slender PE teacher, entered their group. Claire gulped. She was certain this would not go well.

The PE teacher's brows crinkled as she looked down her nose at Claire and Belinda. "That's the rumor going around the school. Girls, social manners requires being kind, especially to newcomers. We want to put our best foot forward. Right?"

This pierced Claire right to her core. She liked Miss Rose. She was a wonderful teacher, and Claire kept up well in her PE classes. What should she say? What should she do? Miss Rose did not understand the Lavender Girls. Maybe she should tell her the truth.

The bell rang, and the chance became lost.

Miss Rose clasped her hands together and bobbed them in front of her. "I trust you will do the right thing." She waved. "Go to your classes."

When the teacher Rose left, Kaye cocked her right hip and placed her hand there. "I guess she told you."

Claire made a decision, a decision which would upset Belinda. "I have decided Miss Rose may have a point."

Her friend sucked in a breath.

With her finger aimed at Kaye, she moved it toward Wendy. "Do not think for a second I won't kick you both out of my house if you cause one little, tiny problem." She got nose to nose with Kaye and narrowed her eyes. "I mean it."

"Ohhhh. You're so tough, Monteiro."

Belinda stepped between them. "I mean it too."

"Let's go." Lizbeth hooked her arm through Claire's.

The BGs entered the room as late bell rang. Belinda's seat was across the aisle and Lizbeth sat behind Claire's.

After class started, Lizbeth's shoe nudged Claire's heel. She lowered her hand at her side and reached. Lizbeth passed a note there. Easing her hand to her lap, she opened the note and read, "I'll be praying for those two girls to act nice on Saturday."

They were going to need lots of prayer.

15

While Claire and Belinda poured their hearts out to Grandma Neecy, Lolly came into the kitchen with her skirt gathered like a basket carrying a treasure. "Looky what I have." The three peered within the bunched material. A few tiny, brown pine cones nestled within the folds.

Grandma Neecy *ohh*ed and *ahh*ed over the cones. She inspected each one, twisting them this way and that as if they were precious jewels. "Whatcha' doin' with them, darlin'?"

"Don't know. They're too pretty."

Grandma Neecy's eyes widened. "I may have an idea." She left the room and went out the back door. When she came back she carried a medium-sized glass jar. "This here is a jar that held a plant. I kept it because I put spare coins in it for gas money." She set it on the table.

The older woman faced Belinda and Claire. "Listen girls. I'm hearing what you're sayin'. I know ya girls are havin' a rough ol' time with Wendy and Kaye comin' to yer school."

They nodded.

"The holy Bible says we're to count our blessings. There's no better time to learn how than when we're discouraged." She took a pine cone from Lolly's skirt. "May I have this one?"

Lolly bobbed her head in quick jerks. "I can get you more, Grandma."

"Good." She dropped the tiny cone into the jar. "I'm counting our being here with the Monteiro's as a blessing." Her soft smile made her cheeks plump as she pushed the jar toward the girls. "This is gonna be yer Blessing Jar."

"Whoa. I love this idea." A shiver crossed along Claire's spine. "But I don't want to disappoint you if I'm too upset to think of a blessing."

"Me, too, Grandma."

"All I'm askin' is for ya to try. Once a day, I want ya to place a tiny pine cone into the jar. Share how ya been blessed. It doesn't matter if ya had a hard day. Count yer blessings, even a tiny one."

Lolly bounced on her toes. "Can I do it too?"

"Of course." Grandma Neecy patted the top of Lolly's head. "You be in charge of having three pine cones ready when the girls get home from school."

"Yes, ma'am, Grandma Neecy."

"Good girl."

"But this won't stop the Lavender Girls." Claire tucked a strand of her hair behind her ear. "I never imagined those two mean girls would be at my house, especially at Belinda's birthday party. They will ruin everything."

"Just remember havin' fun is not always top importance." Grandma Neecy's lips puckered. "No, I don't imagine it will stop them from being ornery. But it will help ya two to count yer blessings. This always pleases our sweet

Lord in heaven." She took a deep breath. "Have ya thought to pray for yer enemies?"

"Grandma." Belinda snagged her grandma's sleeve and tugged. "Ya don't know these girls."

"I beg yer pardon. I was there at the Gallagher Springs school the night Claire got her re-ward. I heard Kaye makin' mean remarks to Dotty." She didn't bat an eye. "I do declare. How ya girls ever, ever gonna share about Jesus if ya don't show them He is in yer heart?"

Claire was struck dumb. She'd never even once thought to show the love of Jesus to them. Not in Gallagher Springs or here at home.

She and Belinda shared a glance. She didn't know about her, but she grew ashamed. Far worse than in English class over the poem and the boys. Far worse than Miss Rose's intent to teach her social graces. "You, you're right," Claire whispered. "I never forgave Kaye for embarrassing my mother and causing her to run away. I almost lost her that night because of that bully. But really, they don't know when to quit." She stared at Belinda's grandma. "How can I forgive if they never stop bullying? I'd be nothing more than a verbal punching bag if I weren't on my guard."

"I've never forgiven them either. And I'll never like them." Belinda inched closer to her grandma. "I'm sorry, but I won't."

Grandma Neecy gripped Belinda's hand with her fingers. "I've lived a long life, girls. If I've learned nothin' else it's this ... when people act out in mean ways, they're usually unhappy." She raised her brows. "Are ya girls happy?"

They nodded.

"And would ya ever for no certain reason be mean to others?"

They shook their heads no.

"Okay then." She lowered her chin. "Think on this, why don't ya. These two city girls are right now drifting through life in the wilds without their mamas." She arched a brow. "At least I'm supposin' they are still without their mamas like they were in Gallagher Springs?"

The girls shrugged.

The old woman spread her hands over her apron-clad stomach. "I wanna give ya a challenge, little ones." She gazed at them. "Tomorrow find out if their mamas are still in Boston. Will ya do that? And report back to me. Okay?"

Belinda's lips parted as though she would speak, but clamped her mouth shut.

"Okay. We will." But did she have the nerve? And how would they take her asking them personal questions? She really didn't need another conflict and one that she would most likely start.

With arms outstretched, Grandma Neecy gathered the girls into a squishy hug. "My youngins. I had my own troubles when I was yer ages. It's a part of growin' into a woman, don't ya know." She squeezed them tighter. "This is when ya make decisions which form what ya will become." She let them go and patted her chest. "Is yer heart right with God?" She turned her back to them and kept working at preparing their evening meal.

Claire stared at Grandma Neecy. Was her heart right? She blinked at Belinda. "I'm not sure. Is yours?"

She bowed her head. "Not sure either."

As she assisted Grandma with supper, she marveled over her words. She always took everything the older woman said as the gospel truth.

But it would be difficult—if not impossible—to act kindly toward the Lavender Girls.

16

Neither of the girls had an opportunity to find out if Wendy and Kaye's moms were with them or still in Boston. They had been absent on Friday.

Claire greeted the party guests the next day as they arrived in groups. Earlier, Grandma Neecy agreed to meet the Lavender Girls when they arrived. It was Claire's idea to establish an adult-in-charge presence. Belinda's grandma had told her that was a wise decision.

Hopefully there would be no problems. She was even praying the Lavender Girls wouldn't come.

Colorful balloons hung from the ceiling and green and white crepe paper was strung around the upper walls of the living room and formal dining room. Pin-the-Tail-on-the-Donkey and several jacks sets awaited players. There would be ice cream, cupcakes, and a sheet cake to follow after the games. Grandma Neecy even made Belinda's favorite raspberry-flavored drink.

Great puffy clouds dotted a blue sky. The sun warmed the late morning and turned the air muggy. She had decided they would move the party outside after the games.

Most of the guests had arrived and were grouped in huddles playing jacks when there was a knock at the door.

Claire's heart plummeted. Grandma Neecy bustled over and opened the door. "Come on in. The party's just gettin' started."

She craned her neck to see even though she was sure who had arrived. Wendy and Kaye walked into the room. Both girls glanced around, noses raised, eyes set as though bored.

"It's your turn, Claire." Lizbeth handed her the jacks and the ball.

She played until she missed a jack, and Belinda reached out her hand to go next. Claire spread her attention in different directions to keep track of Wendy and Kaye. After a while, Belinda touched her shoulder. "Do we eat cake first or go outside and eat cake later?"

Satisfied the Lavender Girls were only watching everyone, she grinned. "How about we take the donkey game outside?"

Belinda jumped up off the floor and raised her voice. "Okay. Girls, listen up. We're taking the Pin-the-Tail-on-the-Donkey game to the front porch."

"Can I play, Sissy Pie?"

"Sissy Pie!" A mocking voice hooted.

Claire pressed her little sister to her waist. *Ignore Kaye.* She gritted her teeth, though, ready to kick her bully behind. *Is your heart right with God?* Her nerves were on edge and peace fled. *I want revenge.*

Still unable to think of how to respond, other wise words came to mind. *If you have nothing good to say, say nothing at all.* Mama always had to remind her and her siblings.

She cupped Lolly's hand and squeezed. "Of course you may play after everyone else." As she passed Kaye, her mouth relaxed, eyes soft and she led her sister outside.

The party guests had the donkey game in place on the porch wall. Lorene stood behind one girl, Heidi, and tied a bandana over her face. Belinda clapped her hands. "Y'all know how to play?" Some of the girls nodded their heads. "If ya don't, just watch Heidi 'cause she has this game at home."

Heidi was spun like a top and then placed in front of the paper donkey target. "Here's the tail." Lorene handed her the tail with a tack stuck at the top. "Now girls, she won't feel for the paper because that would be cheating. Just push the tack into the area where you end up."

She giggled, walked a few steps while her hand held the tail in front of her. She pushed the tack in a lower corner. She missed the hind end altogether. After the other girls played—except Wendy and Kaye who didn't want to—it was Lolly's turn to tag on the tail.

Belinda handed Claire the blindfold, and she wrapped it around her little sister's eyes. She made sure Lolly faced the donkey target.

Kaye sniggered. "What makes her think she can win if no one else has?"

Once more, Claire clamped on her teeth. This time her bottom lip was caught between them.

When Lolly pushed the tack in, everyone clapped. She lifted the bandana, gasped, and stomped her foot. "I missed." She crossed her arms, craned her neck, and cried.

Belinda rushed to her, beating Claire to her side. She lifted her and calmed her with shushing sounds. "Don't cry. Looky. Ya got the tail closer than anyone else to his bow bow. See?"

On the word bow bow, she peeked at the target and sniffled. "Bow bow."

They chanted it together and giggled.

"Whoever heard rump called a bow bow?"

All the girls stared at Kaye. Some of them narrowed their eyes. Others pursed their lips. Pink blotches spread over Kaye's cheeks.

Heidi stood next to Claire. "Don't you two want to play?"

"I think not." Wendy sniffed. "It's a child's game."

Lord, please help me to not speak.

After Lolly and Belinda stopped giggling, Claire thought about ice cream and cake. But she wasn't ready. Instead, she announced to the group of girls. "Let's take a hike on the old logger road behind my house."

Belinda swiveled to the door. "I'll let Grandma and your ma know where we're going."

"Wait." Claire grabbed her little sister's hand and tugged her toward Belinda. "Take her inside. She's too little to hike."

"No, no, no." Lolly dragged her feet and cried all the way into the house.

~^~^~

Claire stayed in the lead and leaned into her climb of the steep logger road. The scuff of shoes lagged behind her. She halted her steps and twisted to check on her followers. Some girls had flushed faces and were drenched with sweat. Other girls only huffed in the sultry air.

The Lavender Girls struggled to bring in the rear. Claire held up her hand. "Let's wait for the others." Kaye stopped, bent, and placed her hands on her knees, while Wendy swung her arms as she kept a steady pace but far behind the crowd.

"Belinda, will you lead them the rest of the way? Just go a little slower, and I'll stay with the lag behinds."

"Ya betcha." She hurried to the front.

Claire walked back down to help the Lavender Girls. When she was within five feet of Wendy, who had stopped to rest, she gestured. "You two okay?"

Kaye gasped for air, still staring at the ground.

"Kaye's too hot and tired. We need to rest."

"Okay." Claire turned and settled on the embankment. "I'll wait." See? She acted kind. Just like Grandma Neecy had asked of them.

As Claire tossed a few pebbles into the trees below, Kaye whined. "No. I can't."

She faced them as Wendy pressed a hand on her friend's arm. Claire rose from the dirt. "You two ready after your short break?"

Sweat dribbled along Kaye's brown hairline. "You are such a show off, ClaireLee."

"Stop calling me that, and I understand you need a break. You don't hike like I do."

"You finally figured out how to outdo us." Kaye spread her arms wide as though taking in the forest. "You are in your element. I'll bet you took us on this mountain to prove you are better than us in the woods."

Brother. Claire rolled her eyes toward the heavens. Oh, how she would love for Grandma Neecy to witness this conversation. Oh, how she would love to abandon these two. She moved up the hill to leave them both in the dirt.

She ignored Wendy's protests to stay with them. She sprinted toward the others and grumbled under her breath. "Suit yourselves. Serves you right. Who cares?" Besides, she figured they'd go back to the house and wait for their ride to come. It's not like they could get lost.

Spoiled babies.

As Claire drew closer to the group of party-goers, excited voices helped her forget the Lavender Girls.

"I've never seen such a view."

"Me neither."

"Is that Saddle Mountain?"

"Looks like it."

"My brother climbed that mountain last year."

She grinned. The girls' excitement had reached her from the top of the wide, flat area. She learned from Daddy that the loggers called this a landing. This was where cut logs were loaded onto trucks to be taken to the mills. But over the decades, brush and trees had grown back on the mountain side. What remained of the logging operation was the road, the landing with brush, and a few smaller trees that dotted it.

Some of the girls sat on an old log and shielded their eyes from the bright sun as they watched the sky in what seemed silent wonder. A high-pitched screech from above told Claire all she needed to know. A bald eagle flew overhead. The bird's head reminded her of a snowball with a yellow beak, perched on dark feathers and ending with a white tail.

Faster than two blinks, the air grew stifling. And the sun hid behind a mass of quickly approaching gray-black clouds.

"Weather's changin'." Belinda nudged Claire. "We best leave. It's gonna gush—"

A rumble cut off her words and came from the direction of Saddle Mountain. Lightning flashed beneath the dark-as-night clouds.

Claire waved at the group. "Let's go." She scurried down the logger road and looked over her shoulder. Three of the girls were in a row, with arms hooked through elbows. They laughed and chattered as they followed. At the end of the line, a few straggled in the back.

Belinda scooped her arm through Claire's. "We sure are havin' fun, aren't we?"

"Yes."

Calm split apart as thunder and lightning struck at the same moment. Plummeted with hail the size of peas, the girls screamed and rushed forward as they slid and fell on the ice balls.

Panic gripped Claire's chest. She waved at the girls as though they were a flock of chickens. "Get to the tree line. Hurry!"

Rods of light bolted toward the earth behind her, lighting the shadows of the earth around her. She rubbed her eyes from the near blinding it had caused. More screams, cries, and high-pitched voices filled the huddled group. Hail turned to rain and soaked them.

Please God, no fires. She could only hope the lightning strike was as far away as Saddle Mountain.

Claire had to think. *Shelter.* She remembered the boulder overhang she and her brothers had found when they first moved to their land. And she thought for sure the rock formation stood in an open space, surrounded by old-growth fir trees.

"We're crossing the road." She guided the group to face a different direction. "There's a cave."

She grabbed the two closest girls' hands and she ran across the road. Belinda hollered but the thunder drowned her words. Behind Claire, lightning struck again. *Too close.* The air sizzled with electricity.

More screams. Howling.

The squish and splats of the girls' shoes in the mud nipped at Claire's heels. She tried to look over her shoulder to count how many followed, but they were a blur in the waterfall downpour.

As they made their way to the other side of the road, two streams gushed along grooves made by vehicle tires. Between the road and embankment they still needed to hop over the V-cut ditch.

"My glasses," someone cried. "I can't see."

"I've got ya." Belinda hollered.

Off the road and higher on the embankment, the group hurried along a narrow trail. Claire halted. Girls bumped into her back. Did she need to go lower?

Or was she lost?

17

"What's wrong?" Belinda stood next to her.

"We need to head downhill."

The group gathered in a circle around their leaders. Hair plastered to their heads and faces, all of them shivered. A few still cried. She nudged Belinda. "Let's go."

She kept away from the road until she spotted the old-growth firs. *Thank you, Lord. Almost there.* The rain slowed to a steady shower. She twisted to count heads. Everyone was there. But. What about Kaye and Wendy? Did they make it to the house ahead of the storm? She prayed so.

As she marched along, the boulder came into view. It was easy to spot because it shot over from a hill creating a shallow cave. Her heart slowed to its normal rhythm. The group moved as one toward the opening, but only a few girls crowded underneath the ledge.

"It's okay." She waved the rest inside. "The cave is only a few yards deep, but still we'll be drier." She led the way into the darkened hole. As Claire sat on the pine-needled ground, she relaxed against a rock. Grandma Neecy would call this rain a gully washer. So relieved to feel safe again, she twitched her lips.

With what seemed like everyone out of the rain, she counted again. "We're all here." She clasped her hands together and thanked the Lord.

Someone said, "Where are the new girls?"

Gulping over a lump in her throat for the two city girls, she had to say something to reassure the group. "They stopped halfway along the road. I figured they headed for the house."

An elbow bumped her ribs. "Ya aren't sure where they are, huh?"

She closed her eyes, unable to look at Belinda.

"Okay, y'all. We need to pray for Kaye and Wendy. We're not sure if they made it back before the storm hit." She bowed her head. "Dear Lord, please keep them safe. Don't let no harm come to them." She elbowed Claire again.

After the short pause, she prayed. "And, dear Father, we hope the two girls are warm and dry and eating cake." Chuckles echoed in the tiny cave. She finished with, "In Jesus' name we pray. Amen."

"Amen" rose from the lips of the teeth-chatters.

The girls on either side of her drew closer and everyone waited for the storm to subside.

~^~^~

The claps of thunder and bolts of lightning moved on, and with them, the rain.

Claire shifted. "Let's go back to the house." With ease this time, she led them to the old logger road in a snap.

Halfway there, her brothers came into sight. They wore hats, rubber boots, and jackets. Liam waved and ran to meet them. "We were worried."

As the boys drew closer, she yelled. "We got caught in the storm. Had to hide in the cave."

Liam patted Claire's arm. "Smart move, Sis." He tugged on Grayson's sleeve. "We gotta get back and tell Mama they're alright. She was about to call the sheriff."

"Did Kaye and Wendy make it back okay?" She nibbled her lip with her question. His frown deepened and panic ramped up her breathing. "What?"

"They're not with you?" He peered over the crowd.

"Uh-oh." Grayson sloshed his boots around in the mud.

She glanced at Belinda, and her friend shrugged. She faced the boys again. "Tell Mama we're okay. The rest of you go with Grayson."

No one spoke. No one moved.

Lizbeth moved next to Claire. "Shouldn't we search for them?"

"Well, yeah." Belinda placed hands on her hips. "But there's no tellin' where they wandered."

"Boys, you stay here." Claire nodded at her brothers. "I need you both. You know these woods. Those who are too cold, go on back and tell my mom we're okay and that we're looking for Wendy and Kaye."

Lorene stepped forward. "I'll go tell your mom."

Heidi stood next to her. "Me too."

The two volunteers continued their trek down the road.

"I say we split into groups as close to equal as we can." Liam stepped closer to Claire. "You, me, Grayson, and Belinda will be the leaders 'cause we know the place. We'll stay within earshot of one another, calling their names."

"Okay." She gave orders as to how to take four groups and walk each side of the road and a few yards into the trees. "I don't believe they would have wandered deep into the forest. They'd be too scared."

Everyone got into groups, spread out, and called the girls' names. Her brothers also whistled in short tweets for them.

She headed in the direction of the meadow where they housed the chickens, Goat, and Bossy. She and the girls with her called and hollered, but no answer. Soon they arrived at a small clearing and spied the hen house and barn roofs.

Her gut clenched. "Where are they?"

The shortcut to the meadow led to a steep embankment. Claire knew this area well. "The rest of you keep walking and head to the house. I'll check below to see if they took shelter in an outbuilding."

The other girls took a deer trail near the road, and Claire maneuvered her way to the edge of the steeper embankment. Below, the stream rushed where before the storm it was dry creek bed. She peered over the side. "Way steep." She took a deep breath. "Here I go." She scooted down on her behind and leaned backward, the incline slick as maple syrup.

A few times, she tipped toward a dangerous roll. She lay flatter and dug in her heels. Near the bottom, the seasonal stream gushed. Not sure why she even cared about getting wet, she let herself slide and hit the stream with a gush. She yelped from the cold as she sat in water up to her waist.

She shiver-crawled up the other side and sloshed in her wet shoes across the meadow toward the cow and goat barn. Bossy and Goat met her at the fence. She patted their heads and peered into the empty enclosure. "It's okay, girls. Storm's over." The animals mooed and bleated.

She headed to the hen house where the door to their pen was shut instead of open. She squeezed her brows together as the wet hens pecked at bugs and grasses.

Claire reached for the rusty handle. A sound came from inside, and she opened the door and gasped. Huddled in an embrace on the ground, Kaye and Wendy shivered and wept.

She made it to them in a few steps. The girls were still crying as their eyes followed her movements. She knelt next to them. "Are you hurt?"

The Lavender Girls did not answer and continued to sob as though the world had ended.

Tears pricked her eyes. "I'm sorry. I should have made sure you got off the mountain safely." The two girls appeared to stare right through her. Were they in shock?

They shivered so hard, their teeth chattered. Claire's heart ached. She wouldn't wish this on her worst enemies. Like them.

She reached out to them and used a soothing tone. "Here, let me help you both to the house. We'll make hot cocoa with marshmallows." When Wendy and Kaye made no move to rise, she wiggled her fingers. "Come on. Doesn't cocoa sound yummy and warm?"

After a long minute, Wendy nodded. Kaye opened her mouth as though to speak, but her teeth clicked. "Come on then." She touched them both on the shoulder. "Let's go. Get you into warm, dry clothes."

The two girls leaned toward her and got on their knees. Several breaths later, they stood.

She knew these girls were as proud as a mountain was tall, so she refrained from saying anything more. She squeezed between them, wrapped her arms around their drenched waists, and led them from the coop.

In slow steps, the three girls walked. She didn't know about them, but scrunching between the two girls warmed her chilled bones. Another thing warmed her heart. Neither Kaye nor Wendy showed anger.

Maybe they could strike up a friendship and forget their feud. Grandma Neecy would be proud.

~∧∧~

As Claire sat on the living room floor, Grandma Neecy wrapped the Lavender Girls in towels. She brought hot cocoa to them as the other shivering girls drank theirs and chatted. A large marshmallow floated in each of Kaye's and Wendy's cups.

They remained quiet, clutching the mugs between their hands. They hunched on the formal dining room floor near the woodstove while Daddy added more wood to the fire. The woodstove hadn't been started yet this year, so it smelled more like dust.

She scooted closer to the Lavender Girls and settled in and sipped on the cocoa she had served for herself. Her other hand held a cupcake. "Did you call for your ride yet?" She took a bite of her cupcake.

Wendy nodded.

Kaye frowned. "Our dads will be furious."

Claire gasped, and her bite of cake lodged in her throat. She coughed. The sweet treat rose to her tongue. As she chewed and swallowed, she narrowed her eyes. "What's that supposed to mean?"

"It means," Kaye leaned closer, "you'll be hearing from our dads." She poked Claire's shoulder with her long fingernail. "You abandoned us. In a wicked storm."

"Are you saying I did that on purpose? Because I did not." She waved her cupcake laden hand. "How was I supposed to know about a storm?"

In the quiet, Wendy sniffed. "It was before the storm when you left us, but still." She sipped her drink. "We weren't familiar with the area, Claire."

She rose from the floor and placed her drink and treat on the dining room table. "I told Grandma Neecy you two would never change." She bent so she was within a breath from Kaye. "You invited yourselves to this party."

"*Kachoo.*" Kaye wiped at her nose. "If I've caught a cold—" She snarled.

Heat crawled along Claire's neck. She was done with this conversation. But it was obvious Kaye's nose needed attention. And just in case Grandma Neecy noticed…. "I'll get you a tissue."

She hurried to the bathroom and mumbled the whole way. "There is no way to change those girls. No way. No how." She grabbed the toilet paper roll and ripped off a long piece. Now as she stood in front of Kaye, she handed it over. "Here."

Her lips parted. She took the tissue and blinked.

She reached for Kaye's cup. "You need more cocoa?" She faked the best ever smile.

She glanced at Wendy and back at Claire. "Uh, sure." She gave Claire her empty cup.

She muttered in her head as she hurried to the kitchen. *I shouldn't be doing this. She doesn't deserve it.* She blew wisps of hair from her face. After she poured the warm cocoa into the cup, she sat the half-full pan back on the cookstove. Pursing her lips, she pinched a marshmallow and plopped it into Kaye's cocoa.

When Claire headed toward the girls, she stopped. Where were they? She stared at their vacated spot. Someone said bye, and the front door closed. She sat the cup of cocoa on the dining room table and hurried to the picture window. Wendy and Kaye were climbing into the backseat of a shiny black car. She grumbled. "Good riddance."

"Who ya talkin' to?" Belinda stood next to her. "Oh. They're leavin'. I heard they're blamin' ya for gettin' stuck in the storm."

"The very nerve." She glanced around at the party goers wrapped in towels in different groups playing games of jacks. "At least the others don't blame me."

"Nah. Ya have some good friends here."

"So why do I feel so bad about the Lavenders?"

"Ya have a big heart?" Her eyes sparkled. "Ya tried, little buddy. Ya really did."

"At least Wendy admitted I didn't leave them when the storm hit, but before."

"That's mighty nice of her." She chuckled. "Come on. Let's play jacks." She grabbed Claire's arm and pulled her to a vacant spot on the wooden floor. She pulled a pouch from her pocket and sat cross-legged on the floor.

"You always know how to get my mind off what's bugging me, big buddy."

"Ya got a nickname for me?"

"It just popped into my head."

The two girls giggled. They played several games, and Claire won every time. Soon, the party-goers left in groups as they had come when they arrived. When the room cleared, she gazed at Grandma Neecy on the floor with Lolly. They played a game as well. Or rather, her little sister was learning. With her long braids and short bangs, Grandma Neecy looked like a bigger version of a little girl. She threw her head back and laughed as she missed a jack. Lolly's giggles ricocheted.

When Grayson joined them, things went downhill like a mudslide. Every time Lolly messed up, he let her know. He would fall backward on the floor in laughter at her mistakes—like when the ball bounced off one of the jacks.

The next time it happened, she yelled. "Not funny."

As the ball disappeared under the couch, Grandma Neecy said, "Grayson, get the broom and fetch that for yer sister."

He did as he was told but by then Lolly had lost interest in the game. Instead, she watched Feather crawl on the floor and pick at cake crumbs and stuff them into his mouth.

"Yucky, Feather." Lolly lifted him. She swayed. "He's too heavy."

Grandma Neecy rescued her by cradling the baby into her arms. "Don't ya be doin' that, doodlebug. You'll hurt yer back."

After Grayson retrieved the little ball from under the couch, Claire took the broom and began to sweep. She started at the pantry area, through the kitchen, and ended in the living room where Mama met her. "Party's over?"

"Sure is." She used the broom to push the dirt and crumbs into little piles.

Mama followed her. "I'm so glad everyone got back safe from the storm."

Frozen in place, Claire stared at Mama. Did she remember who Kaye was? She prayed not. "No worries. Everything turned out fine."

"Well, another thing." Mama wrung her hands. "I feel bad. Soon you'll be put out of your bedroom for Grandmother Walker."

Oh, that. She sighed in relief. Obviously, Mama didn't remember Kaye from Gallagher Springs. Claire stopped cleaning and took Mama's hands into her own.

"Daddy said if she stays longer than two weeks, I can ask Grandma Neecy if I can sleep in the caboose."

She would never tell Mama that Grandmother Walker put her on edge with her bossy voice. What worried Claire the most?

This bully would live with them.

18

"I'll return in three hours." Daddy leaned out the driver's window and kissed Mama before he drove off in their station wagon.

Claire, her brothers, and Belinda stood on the grassy area near the gravel driveway, waving goodbye. Grandma Neecy and Mama, on one crutch now, went into the house.

She kicked at a pebble here and there and regretted what would happen when Daddy returned. Their family would be dumped on its head.

"I swear." Liam grumbled under his breath. "I'll never ever like ol' Grandmother Walker."

"Me neither." Grayson crossed his arms and huffed.

Belinda shooed a fly away from her face. "Ah, y'all. She can't be so bad."

She and Liam chimed in unison, "You wanna bet?"

"Wait 'til you meet her." Liam flicked his fingers at Claire. "Is your room ready?"

"It is." She kicked another rock and sent it into the air. "I've got Daddy's sleeping bag on the sofa with my pillow for where I'll sleep. Mama said Grandmother Walker is cold-blooded and needs my blankets."

Grayson tapped her arm. "Why don't you sleep in the bed with her?"

She snapped her head to stare at him. "Can you imagine sharing a bed with a mean person?"

"Umm, no." Grayson squinted. "That would be like me having a sleepover with Ricky Mullen."

She strolled along the driveway and everyone followed. "Is that the boy who beats you in tetherball?"

"Yeah." Grayson's eyes widened on his heart-shaped face. "And then he bugs me about it for the rest of the day. He says stuff like, 'loser, loser, you're a loser.' I don't like it."

The group moseyed back to the porch steps and sat. She sighed. "I feel that way about the Lavender Girls."

"I'll say." Belinda picked the dirt from under a fingernail. "But ya know, Wendy hasn't called me a hillbilly or scarface."

Behind Claire, the front door opened. Lolly peeked out. "Grandma Neecy says it's time for you girls to fix lunch."

They hurried inside. Claire entered the kitchen first and stood beside Grandma Neecy at the stove. "I'm glad Daddy's going grocery shopping before he picks up Grandmother Walker."

"Yeah, huh." She added browned venison burger into a large pot of cooked vegetables. "We're outta so many food staples."

She leaned into Grandma Neecy's mushy arm. "What can I do to help?"

"Set the table, honey bun." She retrieved a bowl of eggs from the refrigerator. "Belinda, these are already boiled. Make stuffed eggs, please."

"Yes, ma'am." Belinda pulled what was needed from the refrigerator and began her work.

Claire's belly growled. Soup and stuffed eggs sounded good. But what she really wanted was the graham crackers Daddy promised to bring home. For dessert, they'd dunk the crackers in their milk and eat as quickly as possible before the softened treat fell back into their glass. At least that delight would make for a better evening.

Grandmother Walker would find a way to grate on Claire's last nerve.

~∧~∧~

When the family station wagon pulled into the driveway, Belinda, Claire, and her siblings sat in a row on the steps. Laddie sniffed Claire's neck, and she hugged him tight. Then dread rippled along her spine so strong, she preferred to hide in the caboose.

As the vehicle halted across from them, Claire squirmed. Grandmother Walker sat low in the passenger seat, her hair puffed like a white cloud over her crown.

Claire stood and took a backward step as Daddy hurried to the passenger door where Grandmother Walker waited. He helped her up and out, and she hooked her arm into his bent elbow.

Her full height came only to Daddy's chin—he was shorter than all her friends' daddies. She tottered while they walked with careful steps. When she came into full view, Claire stared open-mouthed. Old lady nylons—the kind you couldn't see through—peeked beneath the low hemline of her dress. She knew they had to be the kind with a thick seam. Her ankles were as skinny as a hen's.

Mama had worn stockings like that during a pregnancy because she had painful veins.

Grandmother Walker's hair was shoulder-length with soft curls arrayed about her face. How could such an innocent, sweet-looking, elderly lady be so sharp tongued? Claire and her brothers called her "sword mouth." Well, behind their parents' back. She looked the same as the last time they saw her at the first of summer. She even—

"Now don't go and drop me, Pete." She and Daddy were ready to take the bottom step of the porch. "I'm not as strong anymore."

He took a backward step onto the first and second steps as she stood on the ground. He held her arms. "I've got you, Grandmother Walker."

"Maybe you do." She raised a pudgy foot. "Maybe you don't." She grumbled and muttered the entire way to the porch.

Side by side, Belinda leaned into Claire. "Ugh. She's like a bee in a glass jar."

Claire opened the front door for Daddy and Grandmother Walker, and everyone followed them inside. With Mama taking over to get her settled, Claire drooped with relief into a dining room chair. *We got her in the front door. What comes next?* She closed her eyes and prayed. *Lord, please help. Don't let her get to me.*

"Are ya feelin' sick?" Belinda's breath moved Claire's stray hairs and tickled her cheek.

She pasted on a smile. "Just praying."

"Is she really so bad?"

"I'll never get through this without prayer. Can you imagine living with Kaye and Wendy?" She let her eyes go round. "Well, now you—"

"Aren't you children going to give me a hug?" Grandmother Walker entered the dining room mouth first. She sat and *squeak*. The leather on the seat deflated.

Daddy had taken her two suitcases into what was once Claire's room. Mama opened dresser drawers to add Grandmother Walker's clothes where Claire's had once been.

Grandmother Walker planted fists on her thick hips, a frown creased her soft-wrinkled, age-spotted—grimace?

Claire froze in her chair. Grandmother Walker finagled hugs from her siblings. All the while she hadn't budged. How can you hug someone you can't stand? But if she didn't hug her soon, she'd be getting off on the wrong foot, and it would be her fault.

As she began to rise, so did her grandmother. The old woman walked to her and did the expected. Claire accepted the hug. She smelled of garlic and onions. She tried to fight the urge as she stepped back, but her nose wrinkled.

"Is something wrong?"

"No." She rushed to say, and then said the first thing to pop into her head. "Are you glad you're here?"

"Of course I'm glad." Her frown deepened so that it became scary. "What kind of question is that? I wouldn't have come if I wasn't glad." She looked around. "Who's that girl and that woman beside her?" Her crooked finger aimed at Belinda and Grandma Neecy.

Grandma Neecy reached to shake her hand and offered proper introductions. After chatting for a bit, Grandmother Walker glanced around again. "Where's what's his name? The baby?"

Claire spoke before anyone else. "Feather."

Daddy laughed as the old woman's brows knitted. "Claire nicknamed him Feather. His name is Chipper Frank."

Already exhausted from anxiety, Claire was ready for bed. Her shoulders slumped where she stood. But she no longer had a bedroom to sleep in. Only a place to hang her dresses next to Grandmother Walker's. All her other clothes were stuffed in Lolly's drawers.

She no longer had her own private space.

19

Feather giggled as he bounced on Grandmother Walker's curvy lap. She sang, "Horsey, horsey, go to town. Oops, little horsey don't fall dooowwwn." She eased him against her outstretched legs, and he giggled until he hiccupped. She smiled.

So she did know how to lift her lips upward. Claire hated to break into their game, but it was Feather and Mama's bedtime. She reached for him with a bottle of goat milk in one hand. "Time for bed, Feather."

He shrunk into Grandmother Walker's arms. "No, See."

Their grandmother's knuckle's turned white as she gripped him. "Let him stay, ClaireLee. We're riding the horsey." As though Claire had agreed, she began the game again. The baby laughed so hard he snorted.

She stuffed down her irritation that the old woman still used her full name. But she supposed Grandmother Walker would always call her ClaireLee. It didn't matter what she thought about it. She wiggled her fingers for him to come. "I'm sorry. Mama says so." That ought to make her listen.

"Now, ClaireLee. You tell your mama this baby can stay up. She wouldn't rob me of this precious time, now would she?"

Confused, Claire shook her head no and then she nodded. "Grandmother Walker." She inhaled. *Here we go.* "I will not boss Mama, so neither should you." There. She said it. Nip this problem on the first night.

Grandmother Walker worked her mouth into a wrinkly knot. Ready to argue, Claire beat her to it. "And we can't upset the baby's routine. If we upset his routine, we upset Mama's."

"I'll talk to your mother about this." She held Feather out to Claire, her wrinkles shriveled like an old pumpkin forgotten in the December air.

She took Feather from her and as she moved away she muttered. "I have no doubt."

"What's that you say, young lady?"

"Nothing."She twitched her mouth. In Mama's room, Claire spoke in a low voice, "She's already trying to take charge. What'll we do?"

After she smoothed the blanket over Feather's shoulder, Mama patted his back as he lay on his side and sucked his bottle. "Now Claire, she's an old, lonely woman. We must turn a deaf ear when she gets like this."

She reclined onto the bed next to Mama, and leaned on an elbow. "So you know she's hard to live with." More like an over-the-hill bully.

Mama smiled a slow, sleepy smile. "Oh, yes. What I've learned with my grandmother is to say, 'that's one way to look at it'. Or, 'I hadn't thought of that, Grandmother

Walker'." She held Claire's hand with her free one. "It's easier on her pride that way than telling her no." She closed her eyes for a long moment.

She took that as a clue to let Mama rest, so she got up. "Okay. I'll try it." But she doubted it would work. She bent and kissed her good night and peeked in on the boys and Lolly. It was a school night so the younger kids had gone to bed at seven.

As the eldest with the most responsibility, she could stay up until eight.

One of the boy's snuffle-snorted in their sleep. But when she stopped at her sister's bedroom door, she found her on her back and picking at her fingernails. She sat upright when Claire entered. Claire nudged her back onto her pillow. "Go to sleep, honey."

"I can't." Her lower lip trembled. "I been hearing Grandmother Walker paying attention to only Feather."

Patting her cheek, she smiled. "She does play favorites."

"Is that the game I heard?"

"No, honey." She sat on the tiny bed and smoothed stray hairs from her little sister's face. "It means she gives most of her attention to one person. Some adults do that." She shook her head. "It doesn't mean she loves you less than Feather."

Lolly crinkled her brows. "It feels like it."

Claire thought about this for a moment—she wasn't sure if she understood favoritism. She did know it hurt. "Maybe some people have tinier spaces in their hearts for loving others."

The wrinkle between Lolly's brows deepened.

"What if Grandmother Walker's heart can only pay attention to a few people?" She had no right trying to explain this, and she didn't want to confuse her little sister.

"Oh." Lolly's eyes brightened. "You mean like Daddy talks loud and laughs loud and plays with us on the floor. And Mama," she blinked, "Mama doesn't talk too much and speaks softly and only hugs us." She hugged herself. "I want Mama to kiss me a whole bunch."

"All that is correct." Claire wrapped her arms around her. "You are very smart." And her little sister explained it better than she ever could.

"I know I am." She grinned like she was the most precious child in creation. "Daddy says so."

Warmth spread through her. Little Lolly gave her something to think about. About the cranky grandmothers and bullies of the world, just how small were their hearts? How did they become this way?

As she pondered this difficult topic, she rubbed Lolly's back. Claire kept yawning, but she wanted to help her sister fall asleep.

Daddy spoke, and her ears strained to hear. ". . . stay as long as you want."

Grandmother Walker's voice gave a muffled reply.

"I hope you can sleep well in Claire's bed," Daddy said.

The sound of Claire's door shutting made her heart stutter. *Stranded.*

Still sitting on Lolly's bed after she fell asleep, she hugged her knees to her chest and settled her chin into the cradle they made. So many questions floated around in her brain. Would she ever understand even a small part of what caused some people to react in a mean way?

She needed comfort. Her mouth watered when she imagined a glass of milk before bed. Claire tiptoed out of the bedroom. She met Daddy in the living room on her way to the kitchen. "Sleep tight, ClaireBear."

She smiled at him. "You, too, Daddy." He always gave the best hugs.

~∧∧~

She lifted the gallon jug of milk and noticed the salami and decided a snack would be even better. At the table, she stacked a pile of crackers and sliced salami to go on top of each cracker. As she ate and drank, a soft knock hit the back door. She hurried to open it.

"Hey." Belinda's grin spread across her face. "I saw the kitchen light. But just in case it wasn't you, I knocked."

"Don't knock." Claire waved. "Just come on in."

"I'm thirsty." She filled a clean glass with water.

"Want something to eat?" She lifted the box of crackers and the slab of salami to show Belinda.

Her eyes grew round as dinner plates. "Sure." She settled at the kitchen table across from Claire's seat. "I guess I'm hungry."

"You are always hungry." She settled back into her chair and chuckled. "But you grow as fast as a dandelion weed."

They ate and talked in quiet voices while they enjoyed their snack. At one point, Belinda swiped cracker crumbs from the table into her hand and dumped them into her mouth. "I been thinkin'. You're roomless."

"Yes."

"If the couch is not comfortable, I could ask Grandma if ya could sleep on our sofa. I've sat on it and it is bouncy, so should be comfy." She stuffed another cracker in her mouth and pressed her lips against her teeth and made a silly face.

"Thank you, but—" Claire took a drink of her milk. "It's not that the couch is uncomfortable. I have no privacy." A thought hit and she studied the kitchen. "What if? What if I made this kitchen my privacy room?"

"How can ya do that?"

"The living room is where I sleep." She waved a hand in front of her. "This is where I can have privacy, and only after everyone has gone to bed."

"It might work because everyone goes to bed early."

Claire patted her belly. "I need to eat less at supper so I can snack and not be so full like now. And ..." she grinned, "you can join me anytime."

"Ya know, you're still like one of them chameleons." Belinda tilted her head and chewed on her salami and cracker. "I said it right this time."

"You sure did. No more calling me a 'cameo.'" She brushed crumbs into her palm.

"This is more like ya. Lettin' problems run off ya like water on a hen's back."

"That's becoming harder."

Before Belinda headed back to the caboose, Claire jumped up. "You know what we forgot today?"

She blinked.

Claire got the jar off a small shelf below the wall clock. "Lolly forgot to give us the pine cones, so we'll each have to take one from the jar for tonight."

Belinda reached inside and pulled out a cone. Then Claire lifted one. "I'm blessed because I have a great friend, and her name is Belinda." She grinned and dropped her cone into the jar.

"I'm blessed because I have the best little buddy in the world. Her name is Claire." She dropped her pine cone into the jar.

After Belinda left, Claire slipped into Daddy's sleeping bag on the sofa. She squirmed until the bag came up to her chin. She muttered, "soft and warm," closed her eyes, prayed for her family—even Grandmother Walker—and drifted off to dreamland.

~^~^~

Claire squirmed. Who was sawing wood? Her eyes popped open as the noise grew louder. Though the living room was darker than a storm cloud, she glanced around. No one would cut wood at this time of night. Completely awake, her ears were on full alert.

The racket came from Claire's room. She groaned and pressed her pillow over her face.

She had forgotten how loud the old woman snored. And it sounded like a chain saw, in perfect rhythm.

A giggle rose in her throat. But the next minute doom and gloom interrupted her laughter.

Would she get woken up like this every single night?

20

The older kids raced through breakfast, then grabbed their sack lunches and ran along the driveway to meet the school bus.

Laddie pranced ahead of Claire, and his tongue lolled to the side of his mouth. She would give him her customary kiss on his head for a job well done as was their morning routine on school days.

"Ack." Belinda coughed. "I think a cereal flake stuck in my craw."

"Craw, huh?"

The bus driver pulled along the entrance to their driveway and opened the double doors. Their little group ascended and sat. As the bus rumbled down the highway, it picked up speed with each shift of the gears. Her belly clamped like a fist. She needed to prepare to face the Lavender Girls. She had three classes with them, and that was too many.

When she helped Mama before Grandma Neecy came, it had never exhausted her as much as on the defense with Kaye and Wendy.

"Little buddy?" Belinda leaned close. "Who's the boy behind us a few seats back? He's got red hair and black glasses."

Before she swiveled partway to take a peek, Belinda hissed, "Stop. I don't want him to think I'm talking about him."

"But you are."

"Exactly." Her hands fidgeted on her lap. "What I'm tryin' to say is, I think he's so, so cute."

Someone could have knocked her over with a puffball weed. "Are you serious? Or are you teasing?"

"I'm—"

"Because, Belinda, since when do you notice boys?" She tapped her chest. "I'm supposed to notice them first."

"Who says?" She crossed her eyes. "Is that in some *book* ya read?"

"No. I just figured I'm older by a whole year. Shouldn't I like a boy before you?"

"With your busy life? I don't think you've had time to think about a boy, Claire."

"What do you mean?"

"In case ya hadn't noticed, you're helping your ma every day—even with Grandma and me here to make it easier. And your great-grandmother is here. I'd be flat-out tuckered."

"I do feel tired." She could only pray Grandmother Walker didn't snore tonight.

Belinda elbowed Claire's arm. "Let's look straight ahead for at least five minutes. No talking. Then, ya could look back at Mr. Redhead. After that, we won't talk for another five minutes. And then after that, ya tell me his name and what grade he's in." She spread her hands over her pleated skirt. "This way we won't be obious."

"Obvious. Not obious."

She slapped at Claire's shoulder in a playful way. "Skip the English lesson, will ya? This is serious."

"Okay. I'll take a peek." The perfect opportunity came along. The bus had stopped and more kids boarded. As they passed her, she continued to stare at them, before twisting in her seat. She quickly glanced at the redhead. Within a split wild-hair moment, Claire's heart kicked into full speed. She faced forward. A strange sensation fluttered in her chest … in the exact same area as her heart. *He's gorgeous.*

The two friends sat in silence. All Claire could think was she might as well be stuffed in a pickle jar. Not only was he the cutest boy she'd ever seen—he smiled. At her.

Soon enough, Belinda nudged her. "Well?"

She cleared her throat. "Um, I've never seen him before."

"What?" She *tsk*ed her tongue. "How come ya never noticed?"

"I don't know." She shrugged. "Maybe he's new?"

"You're funny." Belinda bent closer and spoke near her ear. "I saw him the first day I got here, but just now got enough nerve to ask ya about him."

"Two weeks ago?"

"Yep."

The bus made the last curve before the Kerbyville Junior High School.

"Just ya wait and see." She pressed her forehead against the window. "I'm gonna find out all about him."

Claire gathered a book which had slipped off her lap and onto the floor. She didn't want to like him because Belinda did.

As the two friends got in line to leave the bus, curiosity nipped and tugged. She had to glance at him to see if he stayed on the bus. She craned her neck. He sat in his seat and seemed to watch her. She jerked her head forward and hoped Belinda hadn't noticed he smiled at her.

If he wasn't getting off, he was in high school. And since he was on the bus when they got on in the mornings, he must live nearby because there were only a few stops before theirs.

How did Claire miss seeing him?

All through first period class, she could not shoo away the perfect image of the red-headed boy. Who was he? Where did he live? She would find out for Belinda. She would squash her own feelings. Her friend spotted him first.

At lunch recess, the BGs hung around the tetherball court. As they chatted, someone behind them spoke. "What are you girls doing?"

Kaye Tyner.

Claire did an eye-roll. Wendy followed close behind her. "Planning any more parties?"

"Who?" Belinda squinted. "Us?"

"Do you really want me to say, or are you trying to get me to say something wrong?"

Lizbeth touched Claire's arm as in stay calm.

Kaye and Wendy shared a glance. They both shrugged.

Claire tapped her shoe and decided to get something off her mind. "So your dads are angry about you two getting caught in the storm?

"No." Splotches of red dotted Wendy's face. "They're not."

Kaye glanced at Belinda. "We didn't tell them anything except we got rained on."

"Really?" Claire's brows shot toward her hairline. "Why not?"

They both stared at Belinda. Belinda stared at the sky. She whistled. She blinked in a flutter of lashes.

"I see." To keep them quiet had Belinda threatened she would tell people what Kaye said to Mama back in Gallagher Springs?

The Lavender Girls seemed to study the tetherball pole as an active game took place between two boys.

Quick on her feet, Claire took the chance to create another party idea. Not to seem eager, she examined her short fingernails for a long moment. "How about I have a back to school party? It'll be a dance with boys and girls." And maybe this could be a great way to get Belinda and the cute boy together.

All four girls gasped and pelted her with questions.

One side of her mouth quirked. Maybe she was getting somewhere with Kaye and Wendy. Maybe they could all be nice to one another—if not friends. But before she discussed the party any further, she had a question … one Grandma Neecy had wanted answered. She kept a big ol' grin. "Are you girls here with your dads and your maid?"

Kaye's head snapped up. "Why do you ask?"

"Just wondered."

Wendy stared at her shoes. "Yes, well," she cleared her throat, "it's the same as in Gallagher Springs. Our moms can't break away from their commitments to their clubs and social functions."

Claire glanced at Belinda. "You must miss your moms, unless you saw them this summer between tunnel jobs. Did you get to see them?"

Wendy dug the tip of her shoe around in the dirt, making a tiny mound.

"Yes." Kaye glared. "Not that it's any of your business."

Wendy shook her head ever so slight at Kaye and then faced Claire. "Let us help you plan your party."

Lizbeth chimed in. "Each partygoer could bring their favorite record." Her brows rose with her question. "Do you have a record player?"

"Yes, but …" Claire had to halt any more party discussions. She hadn't even asked Daddy if she could have a dance party. "I need to get permission from my parents before we make any other plans."

Everyone nodded their agreement, even the Lavender Girls.

Having a dance party would be the perfect excuse to invite the redheaded guy. Claire would do that for Belinda.

"Does this mean Wendy and I are invited?"

"Sure." She said the next part in a kind voice as Grandma Neecy would have wanted. "But if you two cause any problems, you'll have to leave."

"Us?" Kaye and Wendy asked as if insulted.

Wendy cleared her throat. "I still have my box of various party decorations."

The five girls couldn't help themselves as they discussed the dance party anyway. All the while, Claire hoped her parents would agree.

~^~^~

On the bus ride home, she didn't see the cute guy. Maybe he had football practice?

After supper and before Daddy left from the table, Claire pinned him with a stare. "Daddy?"

"I know that look." He scooted his chair back and stood. "Yes, Claire?"

She swallowed the tiny lump in her throat. "Could Belinda and I host a dance party here at the house?"

He sat his empty plate and glass back down. "A dance?" He looked straight into her eyes. "Honey, I don't know about a dance." He blinked. Opened his mouth. Closed it. Cleared his throat. "When—"

"Now, Pete," Grandma Neecy began, "these youngins' are teens, don't ya know?"

"Go on." Sweat beaded on his forehead. "I respect your thoughts, Neecy."

"Thank ya." She fiddled with one of her long braids. "When it was Belinda's birthday a few days ago, I had to get away and cry a few tears. Now I'm ready to support my doodlebug as she grows into a fine young woman." She splayed her hands in front of her apron. "What better way than to have a party right in their own home? With, of course, adults lookin' on."

Mama gazed at Daddy. She knew Mama had a hard time when she turned thirteen. Did he?

"This is ludicrous." Everyone jumped at Grandmother Walker's words. "These girls are much too young for parties with mixed company."

"Lolly, go play with the baby on the living room floor." Daddy lifted him out of his highchair, sat him down, and let him crawl away.

Mama tilted her head. "What do you mean by mixed?"

The old woman glared at Claire's parents. "You know full well what I mean. Girls and boys dancing together at this age? It's obscene."

"Abigail." Grandma Neecy placed her hands on her hips. "That's enough." Her lips puckered. "Ya have no right to tell me what my granddaughter can and cannot do." Her raised voice was more like a bark.

Claire jolted in her seat. She was always so nice, but this stern outburst was scary.

Daddy said in his most calming voice, "Now Grandmother Walker. Let the parents decide what is best."

She sputtered. Spit flew. The spray landed on her empty plate. "Well. I never …" She lifted her chin and left the table. When she got to Claire's bedroom, she slammed the door shut behind her.

"The old woman's going to break my door." She stiffened at the daring words. She'd be in trouble for sure.

All eyeballs turned her way, but then Daddy gave Mama an "I'm sorry" look. She smiled as though it was okay. He shoved his fingers through the top of his curly brown hair. "Back to what you were saying, Neecy."

Claire's muscles relaxed.

"I said my piece." She nodded once as she stared at Grandmother Walker's empty chair.

"A chaperoned dance is the best way for our girls to start with mixed company." He faced Claire. "I'm giving you permission to have a dance here at our house. Supervised, of course." The girls squealed. "But. You have to clean this place after it's over. Everything back the way it was. Understood?"

"Yes, Daddy."

"Yeah, Mr. Monteiro."

His grin turned lopsided. "Belinda, you can call me Pete."

"Oh. Okay." She stood and gave him a hug around his neck.

"You're a good kid. And I'm happy you are here with us."

"Thanks, Pete." She pulled away. "You're a real fine daddy."

Everyone around the table chuckled.

Daddy and Grandma Neecy left the dining room, while the two girls gathered the dishes. "How many friends do you plan to invite, and when is the dance?"

They stared at Mama. Claire stepped closer to her and sat down. "We're not sure." She glanced at Belinda who leaned against her chair and then back at her mother. "How many kids do you think would fit for a dance?"

"How about twelve kids? That would be six girls and six boys?"

"Oh, but ... could we have ten of each? That way we can include more of our friends." Belinda nodded. What she wasn't telling Mama? Two of them were Kaye and Wendy and that brought it down to only four friends.

Mama twisted in her seat and studied the two rooms again. "You know. We could push the dining room table against the wall because you'll only need it to hold refreshments." She tapped her cheek. "That would give you another four feet of room. We can take the chairs and fill the empty spaces along the walls. Yes that would work. It would also give you eight more places to sit." She grinned. "So, yes you may."

She kissed her cheek. "Thank you, Mama."

Belinda counted. "And with the couch, we'd have four more seats. That's twelve seats. Not everyone will sit down at the same time, if we keep the records going."

Daddy had walk past but then stopped. "Keep the refreshments simple ... like popcorn and punch."

Grandma Neecy gathered a few serving dishes to help the girls clear off the table. "I'll pitch in and buy baking supplies to make dozens of cookies. Just tell me what kinds ya want."

Lolly clapped, "Peanut butter cookies," and Feather squealed.

Everyone chuckled.

"Grandma, please," Belinda folded her hands, "make your cinnamon sugar donuts."

"If ya like them so much … okay."

"Yes." Claire pumped an arm in the air. "We'll have enough snacks to keep everyone happy."

While they washed and dried dishes, the two friends talked about who to invite. The girl list was simple. When they got to the boys, though, that was another matter. Claire scrubbed a cookpot and thought it through. "We could tell the girls to choose which boys they want to invite. That way, it's fun for them, and we won't have to bother with the boy list."

"Smart thinkin'." Belinda swiped her sleeve across her forehead. "It's gettin' warm."

Claire rose on her tiptoes and opened the window above the sink. "Should we allow the Lavender Girls to use their decorations?"

"Sure." As she rinsed the cookpot, water splashed her chest. "I don't think either of us have the money to spare."

"When would the party start and end?"

She stared through the open window. "How about two to five? That way they've already eaten lunch and can go home for supper."

She gave her the thumbs up.

"Um, Claire?"

"Yeah?"

"Let's, uh, let's invite the cute redhead."

"It's up to you who you invite." She stifled a giggle. She'd hoped Belinda would want to invite him. She gave her friend the last of the dishes to rinse and dry. "I sure hope he wants to come to a dance with younger kids."

"Welp." She rinsed the last dish, dried it, and stacked it in the cupboard. "If he's a neighbor, he might." She scratched at her ear. "Right?"

"We need to find out where he lives." She splashed water around the inside of the sink and wiped it clean. "I know. We'll ride the whole bus route on the way home tomorrow."

"Huh?" Belinda wiped dry her counter area. "Why?"

"Instead of getting off the bus when we're supposed to, we'll ride it to the end. The bus driver has to pass our house again on the way back. He can drop us off then."

She nodded. "Oh, now I see." She patted her shoulder. "You're always thinkin'."

After the kitchen gleamed clean and tidy, the girls had every intention of writing invitations on nice stationery. They chatted on the way to Claire's room, but halted at the closed door.

There was no way they could disturb Grandmother Walker in order to get the stationery. Unless, they didn't mind a lash of her razor-tongue.

They minded.

21

Grandmother Walker was an early riser, so Claire planned to wake before dawn. She could sneak into her bedroom and grab her stationery when her grandmother used the bathroom. That way, she and Belinda could begin writing invitations on the bus.

The sun hadn't risen, yet the darkness was lifting, when Grandmother Walker slipped from Claire's room. She waited on the sofa. The pantry door that led to the bathroom made a *swoosh* sound, and she raced to her room.

She skidded to a halt. Her bed was made. A dress was spread out on the bed, along with stockings. Granny shoes sat on the floor by the bed, ready for her to slip her feet into them. Claire darted to her simple desk against one wall and opened the deepest drawer. Light purple stationery with matching envelopes sat at the bottom. Her nana gave her different colors of stationery kits for Christmas and birthdays. A soft purple was her favorite color so far.

Not sure she had enough for the invitations, she opened another drawer where she kept colored paper Mama bought her for Valentine's Day last year. She scooped up several sheets and clutched her supplies to her rapidly beating chest. Her nerves jumped. She did not want

Grandmother Walker to catch her because she knew she'd be accused of snooping.

She snorted at the idea. How could one snoop in one's own room?

Claire swiveled too fast and stumbled, which caused her to drop the stationery and colored paper. She kneeled and gathered the sheets. At eye level, her vision landed on a little box on her footstool. She blinked. Curious, she leaned forward and touched the smooth reddish wood. The box had two leather straps attached from edge to lid. Should she open it? Did she dare? *Do it.* She shivered.

It was never any good when a small, still voice tempted her with those words. It got her in more trouble. But. The box had no lock. It would be an easy peek. She opened the lid and jerked backward at the stench. Her vision blurred. She pinched her nose and studied the oddest thing she'd ever seen or smelled.

A tiny, white jar sat within the velvet-lined box and was filled with something black and flaky. The contents looked similar to Mama's tea leaves, but the smell made her gulp. A wood matchstick was stuck upright in the middle of leaves. She lifted it and a wad of flakes clung to the end. She bent closer and took another whiff. "Ugh." Her stomach pitched like the roll of an ocean wave.

The pad of feet sounded near the door and her hand that gripped the matchstick froze. Did she have time to slide under the bed? She dropped the stick, slid, and barely missed Grandmother Walker's waiting shoes. Her head bumped and hair caught on a spring. "Ow" formed on her lips but she remained mute.

Realization smacked her upside the noggin. If her grandmother sat on the bed, she would sink the mattress and bump Claire. When she got back up, more hair would be caught. She felt for the spring stuck in her hair and worked to slip from its jaws. As the old woman dressed, she understood she had only seconds. A few strands of hair would not come loose, and she did what was needed. She ripped the hair from the spring, and bit her lip against a yelp.

Right at that moment, the springs creaked, and she kept her cheek to the floor. She checked for any space between her head and the spring because when Grandmother Walker got up, any hair caught would go taut.

Her hand moved over space between her hair and the mattress. She let go of a sigh.

Grandmother Walker's feet were mere inches from her. She had bandages on the outside of both her little toes. She slipped her feet into her old lady shoes, grunted as she tied them, and stood. Claire breathed a little easier as this whole mess would soon end.

The clip-clomps of old, heavy shoes headed away from the bed and then halted. "You may come out now, ClaireLee. I know you're under there."

She formed the word, "What?" as a whisper on her lips. Was the old woman guessing? She was sneaky, so Claire remained flat.

"I know you're under the bed because *someone* left the lid open of my chew box."

Claire formed the word "chew?" and scrunched her nose but didn't say it aloud. Curious, she needed to know

172

what that word meant, so she snaked her way from under the bed. She clung to her stationery and stood.

"You were in my personal items."

She wanted to leave, but the doorway was blocked by her aged, boulder-sized hips.

"Did you in fact open my box?"

"It stinks worse than Feather's nasty diapers." She faked a smile.

Her blue eyes glimmered.

Did she think that was funny? Claire's shoulders relaxed. "What do you do with that stinky stuff?"

The older woman's silver brows met in the middle. "It's a type of tobacco, and that's all you need to know." She craned her neck. "And don't be telling anyone I have it either."

"Okay." Claire crossed her arms. "I won't." And she wouldn't because if she kept their secret, maybe Grandmother Walker would be nicer.

The old woman scowled.

"I came in here to get paper for our party invitations." She raised the stationery as if presenting evidence before a judge.

"So." She fisted a hand. "Your father and mother have agreed to this dance?"

Claire stiffened.

She moved toward Claire and walked around her and shut the lid on the box. "It seems to me the respect for an elder's opinion has fallen by the wayside." She sniffed. "I should go back home where I can enjoy tranquility."

Did that word mean calm? She'd have to look it up. Claire unstuck her feet and scurried toward the doorway just as a thought hit her. She turned. "Grandmother Walker? Why do you not respect my parents' say over me?" She spoke in her nicest voice. "Why is it you feel you are always right?"

The old woman's mouth wobbled. She waved her fingers as though flicking a gnat, and she muttered. "Shut the door behind you."

Claire did as she was told and stared back at the closed door. Did she act disrespectfully? Was she being sassy? No. She truly wanted to know what her grandmother thought. And if she'd pushed too far and caused Grandmother Walker to leave, well, okay. If anyone had overstepped their bounds in this household, it was Grandmother Walker.

First, when she defied Daddy. Second, for the stinky stuff she kept hid in the box. Chew must be bad for Grandmother Walker to guard it as a secret.

~^~^~

The two friends invited girls to the party and all responded with yes. A tiny part of Claire regretted having to include the Lavender Girls, but it seemed right. The very thought made her heart lighter. She grew tired of her revengeful thoughts for their hateful ways. Even though she realized kind words and actions would never change Kaye.

She had told Grandma Neecy she'd asked them about their mothers and what happened after. She nodded with a knowing expression. So Claire determined she'd do this Belinda's grandma's way.

The two girls rode the whole bus route so they could see where the cute redheaded boy lived since he never rode the bus home. The bus driver agreed to stop at his house where Claire could add an invitation in his mailbox.

Belinda blew a long breath and leaned into Claire. "Do ya think he'll tell us if he's coming to the dance?"

"I sure don't know."

~∧~∧~

The last boy who had been invited stopped by the girls' lunch table. He agreed to attend the dance and was Claire's partner. Belinda leaned close to her after he left. "If the cute guy doesn't come, I'm okay with not having a boy dance with me."

She was about to answer, but Kaye and Wendy joined them.

Kaye sat across from her. "Are you ready for the party?"

She swallowed the food in her mouth and drank from her thermos. "Almost."

Wendy settled next to Kaye. "We are helping in the school office once a week."

"Doing what?"

"If a student gets a call from home, we write down the message and then take it to them."

"That would be fun." She considered a question to keep the conversation in a positive direction. "Did you ask to volunteer?"

Wendy shook her head no. "A teacher has to recommend students who are doing excellent work and can miss one class a week.

"Because we came from a private school in Boston," Kaye buttered her roll, "we are far ahead of the students here."

She never liked this discussion. She had flunked third grade, and those two girls knew it from back in their Gallagher Springs days.

Was Kaye about to bring up Claire's failure again? Couldn't she understand that would make her uncomfortable? But then, maybe that was the point. Her gut wretched at the thought of the subtle bullying. She glanced at Belinda who had a day dreamy expression. Yep. Probably thinking about the cute redheaded boy.

At the moment, she couldn't depend on Belinda to help stop this conversation.

~^~^~

The two friends settled onto one of the bus seats as close as they could to the cute guy. Belinda's idea and Claire went along with it. She said she wanted to make sure he noticed them. She hoped he would say hi and accept their dance invitation.

She prayed the boy would smile at Belinda and not her. Had she made it clear in his invitation that her friend had invited him? Uh, oh. She forgot to include that Belinda was his dance partner.

She gave an inward groan.

The ride to school dragged. Her hearing intensified as she waited for his voice to greet them.

When the bus arrived at Kerbyville Junior High, the girls stayed seated. Claire didn't know her next move, and Belinda didn't seem to either. But quick as a blink, Claire grabbed her hand. "Let's go."

The girls did not look back and as they neared the bus's steps, someone hollered behind them, "I'll come to your party."

"Look at him and nod."

Belinda shook her head no.

"Yes," she hissed,

She sucked in a deep breath and glanced his way. "See ya tomorrow."

Claire hid a grin and left her friend on the bus. Soon enough, she fell into step next to her. Claire shook her head hard enough to slap her ponytail against her shoulders. "You did it. You made a connection with the cute—"

"Do you want me to bring something besides a record?"

Both girls turned. The cute guy had his head stuck through the open bus window.

Claire nudged her. "Tell him no, just his favorite record."

"No," she waved at him. "Just bring your favorite record."

Jean Ann Williams

And the bus pulled away from the curb and with it
the redheaded guy who may have only smiled at Belinda.

22

"I'm still pinchin' myself." Belinda used her hand like a Scarlett O'Hara lacey fan.

"Because he's coming?"

"Yeah." She whispered within their space in the cafeteria. "So far, boys have only been good for one thing. That's to challenge them in an arm-wrestling match." She stared off into space. Her silly grin wobbled. "Everything's changed, little buddy."

A shadow shuddered over her. He better not hurt Belinda's feelings in any way. Once again, she realized how much their friendship meant to her.

"Whatcha' smilin' about?"

"I'm so glad you're my friend."

"Same here, little buddy."

She finished the chocolate milk from her thermos and wiped her mouth on a napkin. "I'm glad Lizbeth is friends with us too. We're the Better Girls Club, right?

"Yep." Belinda glanced around. "Where's she anyway?"

"She told me this morning she's answering phones while the secretary goes to lunch." She clicked her tongue. "Lucky girl."

"Uh, huh." Belinda winked. "She's another straight A student."

She lifted her shoulders and let them fall. "I'll never get to volunteer at the office. I struggle in math and science, barely getting Cs."

"I don't know the first thing about answering a phone. We never had one before coming here."

For their lunch dessert, each had one of Grandma Neecy's giant chocolate chip cookies from the batches she'd made for tomorrow's dance. Claire stopped munching hers. "I never thought about you not having a phone. We didn't either when we were in Gallagher Springs."

Belinda chuckled. "The Lavender Girls were right back then when they called me a hillbilly." She narrowed her eyes to mere slits. "I just didn't like the way they said it is all." She stuffed the last bite of cookie into her mouth and chewed.

At the mention of their names they arrived at their table, and the two friends shut their mouths. Kaye spoke first. "We're ready for tomorrow afternoon."

"Yes." Wendy drew closer. "I've set aside my decorations that will be suitable for a dance party."

"Bully for ya both."

Claire bowed her head and hid a grin.

Wendy sat down. "What time should we come over to decorate?"

"The party starts at two, so come at one. An hour should do." She did her best to give Wendy a smile. "Thanks." She stood and intended to walk to the nearby trash can to toss her empty wrappers and then leave.

But Wendy touched her arm. "We saw a cute high school student with his head out the bus window. Did he say he'd come to the dance?"

Belinda popped upright in her seat and opened her mouth—

"Yes." Claire lifted her chin. "What about it?"

"I want to dance with him." Kaye fluttered her lashes. "He's a dreamboat."

"What's that supposed to mean?" Belinda huffed. "Another one of your fancy-dancy words? No one knows what you're talkin' about, Kaye Tyner."

Wendy sniffed. "It means he's exceptionally handsome."

"Well, for heaven's sake. Then just say what ya mean." She blew air through her lips, making a rude noise. "Dreamboat, my eye."

Claire was certain she caught her friend trembling.

Kaye tapped her shoulder. "Who is his dance partner?"

Before Claire could answer, Belinda stood. "None of your business."

"It's you, isn't it?" Wendy's narrow brow arched.

Belinda stomped off like a bull ready to ram a fence.

She hurried and caught up with her in the girls' bathroom. "Ignore them. They love to show off." She spoke to her friend's back.

Belinda spun to face her. "They better *not* flirt with him." Tears shimmered within her lashes. Her eyes darted toward the toilet stalls as though making sure no one was around to hear. "I'm not stupid, Claire. I'm no pretty thing.

Not only am I plain, but I've got scars on my face. Scars that scare little kids." She waved her hand down the front of herself. "And I'm way too tall."

She moved to within inches of her dear friend and touched her arm. She wanted to hug her with all her might but wasn't sure Belinda would accept it right then. "You may not win a beauty contest, but you have a sweet and friendly nature. If your guy is too shallow to see it, then he's not worth your time."

Two tears trailed along Belinda's cheeks. She touched one side of her face and whispered, "These scars say I'm ugly."

"No!" Claire threw caution to the wind and grabbed her around the waist and squeezed. "What happened to you could happen to anyone." She spoke into her cotton blouse and the area where Belinda's heart beat in rapid thumps. "You were in an accident. God was merciful when the car hit you and didn't kill you." Her voice came soft. "I would never have known you." Now tears stung her eyes.

"Ahhh, little buddy. When ya put it like that."

She relaxed her hug and stepped back.

Belinda's lashes were still moist, but she grinned. "Let's go to the pine tree."

Before the two girls reached the tree near the playgrounds, a voice called after them. "Hey, wait." Lizbeth hurried after them, and she laughed when she got within ear shot. "Ah, that was fun."

Her friends said at the same time, "The office?"

"Yes." Her grin spread across her cheeks. "I'm suited for it. Maybe I'll become a secretary when I'm grown."

The three BGs arrived at their destination. They sat on the old log with their backs to the school building.

Lizbeth glanced over her shoulder before she spoke. "Belinda, I overheard Kaye and Wendy talking about making sure a certain redheaded boy danced with them the most."

"I knew it." Belinda balled her hand.

Claire shook her head in disgust and grabbed her friend's fist and squeezed.

Lizbeth's face seemed to pale. "Knew what, Claire?"

"It was when you were in the office. They told us in the cafeteria they heard the redheaded boy say he would be at our dance."

Belinda hovered over Lizbeth and Claire. "I'll see to it those two don't make it inside the house tomorrow. I'll, I'll uninvite them at the door."

"Sit." Claire grabbed Belinda's wrist. "You make me nervous." She gave her warmest, calmest smile.

She sat with a loud sigh.

Lizbeth patted her new friend. "Now, don't borrow trouble."

"You don't understand." Her bottom lip quivered. "I like him." She shoved her thumb over her shoulder at the school. "Wendy and Kaye are pretty."

"Just remember they are not here to stay." The bell rang and Claire stood. "And I'll make sure they leave your dance partner alone."

"Me too." Lizbeth breathed the words. Right then, she snapped her fingers. "Belinda Cruz? What if I came over earlier than we'd planned, and what if I brought some of my mom's makeup? Like foundation and mascara and lipstick?"

"Why?"

"We'll get you prettied up before he gets there. Pink lipstick is your color." Lizbeth studied Belinda, while her index finger and thumb cradled her chin as though she concentrated on a potential masterpiece. "The redhead will only have eyes for you. Is he tall?"

"I love it." Claire grinned. "And we don't know if he's tall."

"No matter." She flicked her fingers in a wave. "Just be sure to wear your flat-heeled shoes. You don't want to be taller than him if you can help it." She rushed past them.

The other two ran after her. Claire slid into her seat just before the tardy bell rang.

~^~^~

After class, Claire hurried to her locker for more school books. She heard hardly a word from the science teacher. Not only did science fly right over her head, but she had become distracted. What was she to say to the Lavender Girls? She had no clue, but she would protect Belinda.

The BGs' lockers stood near the Lavender Girls'. She grabbed her two books and tapped Wendy's shoulder.

They both turned, their eyes rounded.

She drummed her fingers on the locker door. "About tomorrow." She prayed silently for more words that would hit home with them.

Kaye slanted her head while Wendy nodded. They seemed eager to hear what she had to say.

She licked her lips. "I will not have any trouble from either one of you at the dance." She didn't blink as she stared at one and then the other. "Because if you give us trouble, I'll tell my dad to drive you home." Her words made her brave and ready for what they might say next.

Wendy waved as though swatting at a mosquito. "We don't plan to make problems for you, Claire."

"No switching. That means you two stick to your own dance partners."

Kaye's jaw sagged.

Claire hugged her books, turned on her heel, and marched down the hall.

~∧~∧~

"Cookies?" Belinda's pencil wavered over her list.

Claire stared at the dining room table. "Check."

"Drinks?"

"Check."

"Donuts?"

"Check."

"Plates and napkins?"

"Check."

Lolly kneeled on one of the dining room chairs and eyed the snacks. She licked her lips a few times, Claire noticed. "Sissy Pie." She tried to snap her tiny fingers as though to get her attention. "Do I get to eat some goodies?"

"You betcha." She reached over and rubbed the top of her sister's head. "Be sure to let an older person fill your plate. Okay?"

"Do I get to dance?" She fluttered her lashes with the question.

"No, baby." She pressed her lips so as to not laugh at her cuteness. "You and the boys are to stay outside while we're dancing."

Grandmother Walker entered the dining room from the kitchen. She *harrumphed.* Her eyes narrowed as she walked past them, and she shut Claire's bedroom door behind her.

"Oh, wee," Belinda whispered, "someone's ticked."

"Just as long as she keeps her mouth closed." She rolled her eyes. "This is not the day to shoot darts at us with her razor tongue."

At a knock on the door, Claire hurried to answer it. Lizbeth entered. She released a soft cloth bag off her shoulder. "I'm ready to apply the makeup." She grinned and glanced around. "Where should we sit?"

Belinda grabbed her free hand. "This way."

They took two seats at the kitchen table where the adults sat talking. Claire stood nearby to watch, and Mama smiled. "Hi, Lizbeth. How's your family."

She dug through her bag and came out with foundation, mascara, and a tiny sample tube of pink lipstick. "Real fine, Mrs. Monteiro."

"Your family is expecting a new baby soon."

"Yes, we are excited, and my mother says she's ready to pop."

"This will make number four?"

"Yes, ma'am." She shook out a dry wash cloth. "May I use your sink?"

"Help yourself, honey."

After Lizbeth washed and dried Belinda's face, she worked in the foundation. Claire placed her elbow on the table and cupped her chin in her palm and witnessed the transformation.

Mama held Claire's other hand. "Are you ready for this, honey?"

Before she could answer, Daddy spoke. "They'll be no kissing." He grinned.

"Daaadddy." Her face burned hot with embarrassment. "Of course not."

"Yucky." Grayson walked into the kitchen from the back porch. "Who would do that?"

Liam followed behind him. "Teenagers kiss, dummy, that's who."

He stared at Mama and Daddy. "I thought only parents did that."

Daddy bellowed with laughter.

"Youngin's got a lot to learn, don't ya know." Grandma Neecy chuckled.

"There better not be any hanky panky going on while I'm here." Grandmother Walker stood in the kitchen entryway, her knuckles on her pudgy hips.

The growl in her words did not escape Claire. She opened her mouth to reassure her, but Daddy beat her to it. "Now, Grandmother Walker. These are well behaved kids. I know that because Claire would only choose them to attend her dance party."

Grandma Neecy eased from her chair and stood behind Claire with palms on her shoulders. "Abigail, I'm assured the girls did as Pete said." Her hands gripped Claire with her words.

Lizbeth tapped Belinda's chin to face her once again but not before she and Claire exchanged glances.

"I saw that." Grandmother Walker's gnarled finger aimed at Claire. "See what I mean, Dotty and Pete, about disrespect? Those two girls are making fun of my opinion."

Daddy gazed at the accused ones. "What?" He scratched his head. "How do you figure?"

Claire walked toward the old woman and gripped her hands together. It was time to clear the air once and for all with Grandmother Walker.

23

"Grandmother Walker." Claire drew closer. "Belinda and I don't mean any disrespect." She stopped within a foot in front of her. "If you want to know why we exchanged looks, it's because you are overbearing about everything and anything. You do not respect my parents' authority as we've been taught to respect them." She gave her mother a glance for her to defend them. "Right Mama?"

Her eyes grew round as walnuts. "Yes." Her lips became a thin line. "I have taught my children to respect their elders."

Daddy stood. "That's right." He moved toward the entry where Grandmother Walker still stood. "Why don't you and I sit on the sofa for a while?" He waved his hand for the older woman to lead. And in his funny Daddy way, he blurted. "Beauty before beast."

Claire hid a grin behind her clamped mouth. When they left the kitchen, the boys giggled.

"Boys." Mama did not bat an eye. "I just now bragged on my children. Will you two make me a liar?"

Both boys stilled and dropped any hint of fun from their expressions. "No, ma'am."

Claire's chest swelled. Her brothers never, ever disrespected their mama.

She nodded once. "I believe you thought your daddy funny, but Grandmother Walker doesn't understand giggles. Especially after what happened, your timing was poor."

"But." Claire touched her arm. "She's never happy, except when she plays with Feather."

Liam took a step. "We'll go outside."

"Yeah." Grayson nudged against him. "We don't want to get in the way of Claire's party." The boys left through the back door.

Mama's gaze followed them. She squirmed in her chair and winced as though her hip hurt. "I've got to lie down."

Claire kissed her on the cheek before she hobbled with her crutch from the kitchen.

Lizbeth stood. "*Tada.*"

Belinda faced Claire. "What do ya think?"

"Oh, Belinda, you are sooo pretty."

"You're joshin' me." But her eyes danced. "Really?"

"Claire, do you have a small mirror so she can see what a wonderful job I did with the makeup?"

She bolted to the bathroom and hurried back into the kitchen. "Here."

"I'll be a monkey's uncle. I do look purdy." Belinda's hand trembled as she held the mirror.

"No, honey." Grandma Neecy swiped at moisture from the corner of her lash. "Ya look like a beautiful princess."

Belinda angled her head this way and that as she stared at her reflection. "I need to wear my nicest dress." She hugged Lizbeth. "Thanks. I feel like Cinderella goin' to the ball." She left the room to change.

Lizbeth tapped her fingers on the table. "Is it your turn, Claire?"

"Not me." She took a backward step. "I don't like stuff on my face."

As Lizbeth packed her bag of cosmetics, there came a knock at the front door. Claire glanced at the clock. "The Lavender Girls." She hurried from the room to greet them.

The first thing she noticed was the light red lipstick on their mouths. Their hair was pulled away from their faces with red ribbons tied around their heads. She looked down. Kaye wore colored tights as she always did, but there was something more. "High heels? You're both wearing high heels."

Wendy reached for a medium-sized box and lifted it. "May we come in?" She carried the box inside. "Where do I set this?" She looked around the room. "Do you want us to begin decorating or do you want to see what we have first?"

"No." Claire pulled out a chair and motioned for her to set the box down there. "I remember how you decorated in Gallagher Springs. I trust you." With the decorations, anyway. She would watch them though. Just in case.

She had already told Daddy about the trouble with Wendy and Kaye. He agreed to take them home if needed. She settled into a chair and sighed. She had the best Daddy ever.

Now if only the party ran perfect with no problems from the bullies.

~^~^~

As the Lavender Girls finished decorating, Belinda elbowed Claire's shoulder. "Hey." She fanned the skirt of her yellow dress. "Am I prettier?" She twirled.

"No."

She stumbled on the last of the twirl.

"You are gorgeous." Claire giggled.

She crossed her arms at her waist. "Lizbeth has the touch."

"She sure does." She fingered her short, puffy sleeves on her dress. "You know, I noticed Grandma Neecy wears foundation. I wonder if she'll let you use hers. That way, you can cover your scars whenever you want. Don't you think that would give you confidence?"

"Yes." She flashed her perfect, white teeth. "I'd be Miss Confident."

A knock alerted them to more party guests. A group of six, three boys and three girls. She told them where to set their records, and to enjoy desserts and drinks on the table.

Belinda whispered into her ear. "I wonder if he'll really come."

"Of course he will. And you're going to amaze him."

The two friends stood at the picture window and watched for more guests. Soon a bicycle rider peddled into the circle driveway. "Is that him?"

Belinda pressed her nose to the glass. "Oh, Claire, he so tall." She bounced on the toes of her dress shoes. "I'm so nervous. Claire? How do I tell him he's my dance partner?" Her mouth formed an O. "I didn't think of that. I'm such a goose."

"Stop worrying. I'll figure out something. Just go. Sit or stand. Act relaxed." She gave her friend a nudge.

Belinda left her spot at the window as the redheaded boy walked onto the porch steps. Claire opened the door before he even knocked. "Welcome to our dance party."

He took off his baseball cap. "Thanks for inviting me, Claire." His record was tucked underneath his arm.

She froze. How did he know her name? She blinked. He blinked back. "Oh, yes, you got the invitation with my name on it." Now she was blurting her words, and she opened the door wider for him to enter. He was much taller than head and shoulders above her height. In fact, she stood eye-level to the second from the top button of his shirt.

Just right for her tall friend.

She cleared a giggle from her throat. "I want you to meet your dance partner."

He followed close behind her. "Dance partner?"

She rolled her gaze to the ceiling. Second blunder. "I forgot to mention it in the invitation. The girls chose who they would invite for their partner." She winked at Belinda as she drew nearer. Her eyes grew wider by the second. Claire stared up at the boy. "I'm sorry. I forgot to ask your name."

"Andrew." He twirled his ball cap. "Folks call me Drew."

She pressed her mouth to tame a smile. Was that a soft look he gave Belinda? She had so much confidence about this. "Drew, this is Belinda Cruz. What's your last name?"

He lowered his lids as though shy. "McAndrews, if you can believe it." He kept his head bowed at an angle, peered at Belinda under his long bronze lashes.

Her heart skipped a beat at the scene. But her friend made gasping noises and interrupted the tender moment. Her outspoken friend had obviously become tongue tied. "It's a very nice name," Claire said. Drew McAndrews. It has a certain royalty ring." She had to salvage the introductions. "Don't you think, Belinda?"

In the serious manner of reciting a vow, she gasped, "I do." Now she sputtered. "I mean, yeah." Her face flushed to a shade darker than the pink lipstick on her full lips.

"Okay, then." Claire clasped her hands together. "You too mosey around, and I'll get a few records on the player." Drew handed her his record, and she left them alone.

At the record player table, she sorted through the choices. She read the label by Johnny Cash. "I Walk the Line." She started the song and turned the volume on high.

Kaye and Wendy slid next to the record table. Kaye raised her voice above the song and chattered like a magpie. "Are there more kids coming?"

She counted. "We still have two more couples and my dance partner." She frowned. "Where are your partners?"

Wendy glanced at a few dancers who took to the floor.

Kaye said, "At the last minute they backed out."

"Why?" And why did she not believe her?

Kaye leaned closer to Claire. "I think they were scared of us because we're sophisticated." She flapped her hands. "You know how boys are at this age. Im-ma-ture. And they always—"

"Liar."

"Me?" She smirked.

Right then, Wendy turned her back on their huddle as though something more important caught her attention.

"I should tell my dad to take the both of you home." She tapped her shoe as emotions of anger built within her chest.

"Oh, so you're a daddy's girl?" Kaye looked down her pointy nose. "You'll never know for sure if what I said about our dance partners is really true, now will you?"

"Maybe no. Maybe yes."

"Who made the donuts?"

Claire's brain stuttered by the sudden change of topic. And doggone it that Daddy was busy on the apartment for Grandmother Walker. But she wanted her room back sooner than later so she would handle this girl's lie.

Kaye pulled a donut hole from the pocket of her sweater. "They are heavy. But tasty." She popped it in her mouth, chewed and stared at Claire.

A bitter taste crawled along her throat. She could see Wendy had tamed down some. Not Kaye. Not one teeny, tiny bit.

24

The song ended and there was another knock at the door. Claire found it a good excuse to walk away from Kaye Tyner. Either that or smash a life-sized donut into her face. That would make her feel good. But at that idea, she thought of Grandma Neecy. Shame filled her whole being.

The last kids had arrived, and the party was in full swing. Couples danced to Elvis Presley's "Hound Dog." Claire looked around for Belinda and Drew. She peered into the kitchen and found them next to the wood cookstove chatting. Because there was no need for a fire, they used the stove as a table for their refreshments.

She took a backward step and bumped into a body. Jimmy Hawks. Her dance partner.

"I thought you might want to dance?" His whole face brightened.

She followed him to the center of the room. The music changed, playing a Johnny Mathis song, "Chances Are." This record was Mama's, and she got permission to play it. Jimmy took her hand and placed his other fingers to the middle of her back. They danced to the slow, slow song.

Two tall figures walked into the room. Claire couldn't help but grin. She'd never seen her sweet friend so sparkly. When they came close enough for her to hear, Belinda's laughter sounded like a tingle of chimes.

She glanced at the floor, heart swelling for her best friend's happiness. Jimmy chatted, but she only heard the tone of his voice and not one word. She just nodded. The song ended. Couples separated, and she spotted Drew and Belinda a few feet away.

Oh, no. The Lavender Girls stood next to them. Another song came on, and Jimmy took her hand. He guided her into a slow dance to the Everly Brothers' "Dream, Dream, Dream."

All the while, Claire alternated between keeping track of Belinda and Drew and the Lavender Girls.

Suddenly, Kaye approached Belinda and appeared to tap her on the shoulder.

Claire squeezed Jimmy's hand in an attempt to make a fist. He stared down at her with a loopy smile. *Whoops.* Did he think she flirted?

Kaye tried to pull Belinda aside, but Belinda being so much taller, shrugged off her hand. Belinda danced Drew away from the bully.

Claire said aloud, "Way to go, girl."

Jimmy bowed his head closer to hers. "You said something?"

"Nothing important."

Kaye cupped her hand to Wendy's ear, and Wendy nodded. Kaye stepped back and watched Belinda and Drew, while she twisted her mouth into a knot.

Lizbeth danced nearby with her partner. Like Claire and Jimmy, they were not talking. Actually, the only couple who seemed to chat was Belinda and Drew. He kept turning an ear to hear what she said. She did likewise to Drew. At one point, they laughed.

Belinda was the most outgoing girl there. But Drew McAndrew seemed equally so. He appeared so much more mature than the seventh grade boys they had invited. Was that it? She gave an inward nod. In what high school grade was Drew?

When she became interested in a guy, he would be older. Wiser. Handsome like Drew.

~∧~∧~

After the song "Dream, Dream, Dream" Claire put on another record and scanned the room. Wendy was hunched over her party plate. Claire stopped next to her. "Having fun?"

She shrugged and stuffed another bite of donut in her mouth. After she chewed and swallowed, she wiped her mouth with a party napkin. "Better than sitting at the house, watching the trees grow."

"You don't like it here?" She poured herself a cup of red punch. "I mean here in Oregon?"

"No." Wendy gazed at her. "I didn't like Gallagher Springs either." She moved a wisp of hair from her cheek. "I'm bored." She snatched another donut and bit off a chunk.

"Why are you here then?"

She stopped chewing, her mouth still full. Her lashes fluttered. It seemed to Claire she made a decision. She stuck her index finger in the air as in signaling her to wait. She finished the bite of food, wiped her mouth, and laid the rest of the donut down. Her eyes searched Claire's face for a long moment. "If I tell you something, you must keep it to yourself."

"Okay." She began to cross her heart as she had done many times before. Her hand froze on her chest. "I don't need to do that anymore. I'm not in elementary school."

"No. You're not." She cleared her throat and glanced around. "My parents are getting a divorce." Her shoulders drooped.

"That's so sad."

"Not only are they divorcing, but my mom left." She stifled what sounded like a moan. Her tears shimmered but did not fall. "I," she gulped as though she had a knot in her throat, "I'm still in shock." Her gaze held Claire's. "How could Mother do this? No warning, except for leaving me a note." Her chest heaved. Her mouth trembled. Blubbering sobs escaped her bow-shaped lips.

She grabbed the bully's elbow, led her away from the crowd, and outside on the front porch. Her heart pinched for Wendy. It didn't matter if she could not trust the Boston city girl.

They settled on the steps. Wendy shared her story about how hard it had been since her mom left. Claire knew about a hard life, especially back in Gallagher Springs where her mother was so sick.

"I don't know what it's like for a mother to physically leave. But I know what it's like for a mother to stop being a mother." Despite the girl she sat next to. Despite all the bullying Wendy had participated in. Claire slung an arm around her shoulders.

Between her loud sniffles, Wendy slumped over her knees. "You do?" She sobbed and continued to blubber incoherent words.

She waited for her to calm. Held her hand. Patted it. After Wendy's sobs were only sniffles, she took this moment to speak again. "I couldn't understand what you tried to say to me."

"It's Kaye." She released a shuddering breath. "She came to this town with me only because I had to come—Dad said he needed to keep me with him." She cupped a hand around her mouth and whispered in Claire's ear. "He was afraid Mom would come back and steal me while he was gone."

Whoa. She wanted to ask the question about how a parent could steal their own child. "So." She clutched both hands on her lap. "Kaye came with you because you are best friends?"

"Yes. No." She slipped a hanky from her sweater pocket. "Kaye's dad pressured her to come with us, so she's not happy these days either." She dabbed at her tear-streaked face. "The thing about Kaye is she isn't sympathetic. If it's not happening to her, she doesn't understand."

"That stinks."

"At first, I cried in front of her. But I've learned to hide my emotions."

"What kind of friend is that anyway?"

"Not a caring one." Her voice became soft. "I've learned a lot since Mom left. Being kind to others has been one of my hardest lessons." She leaned her elbows on her thighs. The two girls' faces were inches apart. "And wealth will not make me happy."

A chuckle traveled up and into her throat. She swallowed it down. "I wouldn't know a thing about wealth."

"But." Her brows knitted. "I thought you were well off."

Claire forgot about that lie—the one she told to the Lavender Girls back in Gallagher Springs. Her face grew warm. "Ummm, no."

"You lied?" Wendy eyes grew round as a party plate. "I thought you never told lies."

"My grandparents are rich." She licked her dry lips. "They help us when needed."

"It doesn't matter anyway." Wendy whispered, "Nothing seems to these days."

The front door opened, and a few kids poured outside. They laughed and giggled as two cars pulled to a stop near the porch steps. "Thank you, Claire," someone said. "We had fun," said a couple of girls.

When the cars left, she stood. "You ready to go back inside?"

"Yes." Her face seemed to shine a bit. Her eyes held a glimmer. "I need to take down the decorations."

Another record played and someone cranked up the volume. She knew this song, a fairly new release by the Everly Brothers, "Cathy's Clown." She walked over to the record player and turned it down. She glanced at two people against the wall. Kaye and Drew. Her muscles became ridged as a statue.

Jean Ann Williams

Where's Belinda?
Wendy went over to them and spoke.
She had to find her friend.

25

Before she reached for the caboose door handle, Claire knocked.

Grandma Neecy met her and the older woman's sad expression told it all. "She's upset." She moved aside and Claire passed her.

The sound of muffled cries led her to Belinda's bed. She touched her shoulder.

"Go away." She murmured.

"What happened?"

She gazed at her. Her cheeks were cherry red and damp. "I'm gonna beat Kaye Tyner within an inch of her life." She bawled all over again. "But ... didn't want ... Drew. I didn't want him to hate me for having a mean heart."

Harsh. Bold. Desperate words. Claire shivered.

"Who am I kidding?" She bowed her forehead into her fisted hands. "I'm no match for Kaye with her little figure and syrupy smile that hides her evil."

She sat next to her dear, broken friend. She cupped her hands around Belinda's. "Don't even start." She moved strands of tear-soaked hair from her face. "It'll make you feel worse." She squeezed her fists. "Not everyone can be petite.

Or tall. Or skinny. Or chunky. God makes us the way he decides. Besides, you don't want to be evil like her."

Her friend sniffled. "I hear ya, little buddy but I can't help how I feel."

Claire scooted closer to her friend until her hip touched her side. "You have the most beautiful blue eyes. And Lizbeth's makeup did a great job. I'll bet Drew didn't even notice your scars underneath the foundation." She tipped her friend's chin so she'd face her. "I don't see them, except for where you washed it away with your sobs."

She giggle-cried. "Ya talk big for such a squirt. Looky there. Your feet don't even touch the floor."

Relieved she sounded better, Claire became even bolder. "Are you going to let Kaye take him from you?"

She pounded a fist on her palm. "No, sir."

"Then come on. Dab at your foundation to cover the scars, and let's go back and put Kaye in her place."

Grandma Neecy talked to Claire in a hushed voice as Belinda worked on her face. "You sure have a way with my girl."

"We trust each other and I love her, Grandma."

Belinda appeared next to them and turned her cheek. "Did I cover the streaks?"

"Yes, except right here." She took her pointy finger and smoothed an area near her chin. "There. You're not going to beat up Kaye are you?"

"Suppose not." She hugged her grandma. "I'll be okay."

"I know, darlin'." Grandma Neecy patted her back. "Yer my tough gal."

As the two friends entered the house, laughter erupted somewhere inside. In the dining room, Drew, Kaye, and Wendy stood at the table. Belinda headed straight for the group, and Kaye lifted her chin. Her mouth puckered like she'd eaten a sour apple.

Drew turned toward the hosts. "This has been a great party." He shook Claire's hand. "Thanks for inviting me."

Kaye hung on his other arm. "Yeah, I'm so glad I've gotten to know Drew."

Belinda stiffened beside her and she gave her a nudge of encouragement. Belinda cleared her throat. "You've been here only a few months, right, Drew?"

Kaye opened her mouth. "He—"

Claire rushed in and stole words from her. "Where did you come from, Drew?"

"Oklahoma."

"Are you here because your dad's working on the tunnel crew?"

"Yep." His grin plunked Claire off guard for a second. He said, "My dad is a flagger to keep traffic from the new road to the tunnel site. In case you didn't know, people will just go exploring." That grin again.

"My dad—"

"What about at night?" Claire cut off Kaye in one heartbeat. "Does your dad set up the road block?"

"Oh, no, a smaller tunnel crew works midnight shift, so another flagger takes my dad's place. He and my dad split the twenty-four hour shifts."

"My dad's on the dynamite crew," Claire began, "to break apart the mountain where the road will go through."

"My—"

"I'm not here because of the tunnel." Belinda grinned at him.

He moved away from Kaye and closer to Belinda. "I noticed you get on the bus with Claire, so where do you live?"

Belinda slung an arm around Claire. "With my buddy."

By now, Kaye snarled and crossed her arms. If anger were fire, Kaye's ears would be billowing smoke.

"Y'all live in a nice place." Drew looked around. "Is it historical? I noticed the wood cookstove."

"It sure is." Claire relaxed as the conversation headed in the right direction.

Belinda moved closer to Drew. "My grandma and I live in a caboose out back."

"Fascinating." He lowered his head to stare at her and didn't bat an eye.

Her belly rumbled with giggles. Her friend had taken the reigns and was leading them back on course.

"It's real cozy. Just right for two people." Belinda and Drew were standing next to each other now. "Do ya wanna to take a tour?" She batted her lashes? Claire stuffed down a full-on chuckle. "My grandma's in the caboose right now, so ya can meet her."

His fingers touched Belinda's elbow and she visibly relaxed. "Would she mind, Belinda?"

This cinched it. Those two were a perfect match.

Kaye stepped closer. "But—"

"Nope. Not one bit." Belinda slid her arm through his and took the leading step. "Come with me, Drew McAndrew."

The two love bugs walked into the kitchen and disappeared. Claire sighed. Belinda did it. She gained his attention once more.

Kaye stood next to Wendy and tapped the tip of her high heels in a furious motion. "You know, Claire, it's beyond rude to interrupt someone."

She bent nose to nose. "And you know, *Kaye*, it's rude to attempt to steal a girl's partner." She scowled. "You're so pathetic." She straightened to her full four foot eleven and three fourths height. "How do you like that for the truth?"

She growled something unintelligent and stormed toward the decoration box. "Let's get this done, Wendy. I'm outta here."

The wrinkle between Wendy's brows shot up to meet her blonde bangs. "Our dads should be here soon anyway." She shrugged at Claire and pulled down the crepe paper.

Claire grabbed her arm. "Come outside with me for a minute." Once there, she faced Wendy. "Listen. This is too serious. You need to tell Kaye to leave Drew alone because Belinda likes him a whole lot."

"I'll try to talk to her." She quirked the side of her mouth. "Like I told you earlier, she no longer listens."

"Just so you know. Kaye will be sorry if she ever flirts with him again. I honestly don't know if Belinda will listen to me about not beating her up."

~\^\^\~

Crumb-littered platters in her hands, Belinda's voice grew animated. "We should make a bed on the floor of the living room. I have so much to tell ya about Drew."

"We still have to wash and dry dishes." They passed each other in their cleanup chores. "You're in love, big buddy."

"Yep. Sure am." She filled the sink with water, squirted in some dish soap, and swished the water around to make suds. She hummed out of tune, and that made Claire grin. "Ya know, little buddy, the first time I saw him, I think I fell in love. And now I know he's so nice."

With both hands, Claire stuffed down the trash inside the can they kept in the kitchen. "Yes, he is."

"Is it possible the sayin' 'love at first sight' is true?" She turned off the water. "What if he doesn't like me as much as I like him?" She touched her chest. "I don't think I could bear it."

"Be yourself. He'll like you."

Belinda rambled on and on, and she nodded and smiled. Before they left the now-tidy kitchen, the two friends brought down the pine cone jar. Claire pulled a cone from her pocket. "I'm blessed by my parents allowing me to have a party." The cone pinged against the jar after it fell from her hand.

Belinda held her cone over the middle of the jar. "I'm blessed to have had my first dance with the first guy I ever liked. Loved?" After she released it, the pine cone settled as it rustled on top.

The two friends squealed.

~∿~∿~

Later, after dressing in their pajamas, the girls lay on their backs on the living room floor. Claire peppered her with questions and thought of another. "What grade is he in?"

"He's a sophomore." She yawned. "Not too much older than me."

"No, he's not. So he's how old?"

"He just turned sixteen."

Readjusting a wrinkled cover that poked her shoulder, she wiggled into a more comfy position. "I'd rather have an older boyfriend."

In the half dark, Belinda twisted to face her. "I saw ya with a pretty good lookin' boy, Jimmy, isn't that his name?"

"He's nice enough." She harrumphed. "Problem is I think he likes me too much."

"Ah, come on." She chuckled. "Let's have boyfriends at the same time."

"Why? At the rate you're going, you'll be married before you graduate high school."

She poked her friend in the side. "Don't tease."

"Do you think Drew will ask you to be his girl?" She exhaled as she became drowsy.

"I'm hopin'."

"I hope with you." She yawned.

Right as she drifted into dreamland, a tap on her shoulder roused her. "Are ya asleep?"

Her eyes shot open. "Uh-huh."

"Oh, sorry, little buddy. It's just I have to know."

"Know what?" Her voice sounded like a burping frog's.

"Do ya really believe my eyes are pretty?"

"Of course." Wide awake now, she coughed to clear her throat. "I don't say things just to make you happy, although, I want you happy." She turned on her side to face Belinda's silhouette. "But I will speak the truth to make you feel better."

She patted Claire's head. "You're a good little buddy."

"The way you touched my head, I thought you were going to say I was a good little pet." Both girls giggled into their pillows.

A loud noise drilled through Claire's closed bedroom door.

"What in the world?"

"It's Grandmother Walker."

"You've got to be kiddin'."

"Nope."

"Grandma Neecy does that but not so loud." She yawned. "I'm used to, ummm—" Her soft snores finished her sentence.

Now she was not sleepy. She pondered on events of the day. Would Kaye cause more trouble over Drew? Is Wendy going to become nicer? Jimmy's face came to mind.

Claire sure hoped he didn't get any ideas just because he had been her dance partner.

26

"Who told ya that?"

Claire rushed to stand between her two friends. She pushed Belinda back a step. "Let her explain."

On the school yard by their pine tree, Lizbeth intertwined her fingers near her waist. "Well." Her lashes fluttered as though to clear her thoughts. "Mary and Heidi said they heard Kaye tell Wendy."

"Stop right there." Belinda made a rude noise in her throat. "I don't care for 'she said this and she said that.'"

Claire touched her friend's ponytail and whispered, "She's only trying to help."

"I don't want to hear none of it."

"Okay." Lizbeth shrugged and turned toward the school building. "Don't blame the messenger."

"I didn't mean—" Her eyes widened. "I mean, I'm sorry I grouched at her. Honest, Claire."

"She forgives easily," she said as Lizbeth disappeared around the corner. "She's just hurt right now."

"Dadburnit, anyhow." She kicked a rock near her shoe. "Me and my mouth. But now I need to pay Kaye a visit and confount her."

"I think you meant to say confront."

"Yeah." She soft punched Claire's arm.

"I figured out something about you."

"What?"

"When you get upset, you mispronounce words." She stared at her frustrated friend. "Should I go with you to talk to Kaye?" She hoped she would say no. She was tired of the drama. Weeping Wendy. Stealing Kaye. Crying Belinda. Now Kaye, again. It would tire even Grandma Neecy, she was sure.

"Okay, little buddy." She stuck a thumb to her chest. "But I'll do all the talkin'. This is my bone to pick." She wrinkled her nose. "She won't get by with going after my hopefully boyfriend."

She waved Belinda on. "Lead the way." *This could get nasty.* With that thought, her legs weakened and she dragged her feet.

After searching the school for the Lavender Girls, Belinda raised her hands. "I give up. Where are they on this green earth?"

Laughter came not more than twenty yards from behind the school's tool shed. She hurried to keep in step with Belinda as she marched toward the familiar voices.

Belinda disappeared round the corner of the shed. "What's so funny?"

"None of your business, Cruz."

Kaye Tyner.

Claire followed Belinda but then halted. Kaye stood next to the shed with a toothpick between her teeth. Her eyes squinted as though in defiance.

The silence of the moment roared in her ears.

Wendy lowered her gaze and picked at the grass where she sat a few feet from Kaye.

Belinda stared, drop-jawed. On the tool shed wall, painted in red bold letters inside a red heart: "D.M. is K.T.'s."

One hand flew to her mouth. The other reached for Belinda. Nerves abuzz, she forgot to not interfere, forgot she was tired of drama.

Belinda shook off Claire's hand with a fierce shrug, charged Kaye, and shoved her backward. Hard. Again. And again. Kaye hit the ground and rolled end over end and landed on her back. She sucked in air and wheezed.

Her giant friend stared down at the little bully. "Why, ya evil heathen." She huffed and her chest heaved.

Claire trembled. What should she do to stop this? What if Belinda did something worse? She had to act. Say anything. "Please, big buddy. What would your grandma say?"

She twisted ever so slow. Hurt pooled within her blue, tear-filled eyes.

Wendy tapped Belinda on the back. "Let me have her and we'll leave."

She gave Wendy a sideways glance. "She's not gettin' off so easy. For all the times she called me hillbilly like I was no better than dirt." Belinda snapped her fingers. "She's the low life, tryin' to steal Drew. *She* could have any boy she wanted." Her hands clinched.

She told herself to move before those big fists hit their target, but Claire stood frozen.

"Come on." Wendy dropped her hand from where she had settled it on Belinda's back. "I'll even get the janitor, and he'll repaint the wall. Or I will. I'll make this right. I give my word."

"Your word," she snapped, "means nothin'." She faced Wendy and poked her in the chest. "I've had a belly full of you two." She spit on the grass near Wendy's shoes.

Kaye moved and sat upright and sucked in air.

Wendy's eyes grew round, and she grabbed Belinda's arms. "Listen, I'll make sure she stays away from him. I won't let her find where he lives." She clasped her hands near her heart. "Please."

"I heard about that." Belinda stood a bit taller. She directed her next words at Kaye. "I saw him first, ya little snake. Ya will stop even thinkin' about him. If ya don't, I will follow through with my threat to tell everyone in school what you did to Claire's mama back in Gallagher Springs. And I'll whoop ya good to boot." She bent over Kaye again. "And I hear tell, everyone in these communities love Mrs. Monteiro."

Kaye stared wide-eyed at Belinda, her breath in fits.

Belinda kicked at the ground near Kaye and scattered dirt on her dainty lap. "Do I make myself clear, heathen?"

Her mouth wobbled. "And just how . . . would you tell on me?"

"Ya would ask." Her eyes narrowed. "I will write a detailed letter about that night of Claire's award ceremony. Make copies of it. Give one to every student in junior high."

Wendy gasped. Kaye stared at her without a blink. Claire's brain stuttered. Her knees went limp. Could she talk her out of doing that?

Belinda grabbed Kaye under the arms and lifted her to standing. Wendy steered her away without a backward glance.

After long silent moments, Claire moved to the wall. She touched the lettering and it smeared. She sniffed. A perfume scent clung to her fingers. "Lipstick."

Belinda cupped dirt from a gopher mound against the shed. She spread it over the lettering. Claire scooped and did the same. It did little to cover the initials and the heart. Belinda slapped a hand at the wall. "Forget ya."

The bell rang, and the two friends headed for the back double doors of the school and wiped debris from their hands. "Do ya think Kaye will tattle?"

She hooked an arm through Belinda's. "I think she knows you meant every word."

She halted.

"But I don't believe you have to use any of the threats, especially about my mama."

"Oh. I see." Belinda pulled her arm from hers. "I would never want to hurt your mama, Claire."

"Here's another reason why it's unnecessary. Just the other day I heard a rumor." She continued to walk. "Kaye has all along been inviting girls into their club. They turned her down. Every last one of them."

"Really?"

"She even asked Lizbeth. The rat. So if she tells? The Lavender Girls will be shunned. No one will invite them to a birthday party, or the theater in Cavern Junction, or to go roller skating in Wonder Pass. They'll be outcasts for the whole school year."

Belinda opened the double doors which led to the hall of classrooms, and said nothing more about it, except, "Huh."

A shadow crossed over her heart. She hoped and prayed Belinda wouldn't *accidently* say anything about Mama and that long-ago school night in Gallagher Springs.

27

After she started hot sudsy water in the sink, Claire washed the jars she'd just used to milk Bossy. Grandma Neecy would sterilize them later. She patted Lolly's head where she kneeled in a chair at the table. "I need to look for Belinda."

Moments later, she peered inside the open door of the caboose. The two grandmothers were sipping from tea cups at the dinette table. Grandmother Walker's expression seemed calm, and Claire stepped inside. "Do you know where Belinda went?"

"Hi, darlin'." Grandma Neecy waved at her. "We needed more peanut butter, so she walked to the little store. She said she knew the way because y'all pass by there on yer way to school."

"I'll go meet her."

"How far is the store, anyway?"

"About a mile."

"Well, would ya tell her to buy me some face cream too?"

She would finally leave the house for a while. And one of her favorite things was the walk to and from the little

218

store. She kept a steady pace on the shoulder of the road. Soon she neared the little store and spotted her friend.

"What are ya doing here, little buddy?"

The two friends met. "Your grandma sent me to buy face cream. Why didn't you wait until I finished milking? I could have gone with you." They turned back toward the store.

"Well. I … Ya see ... Drew and I agreed to meet at the store whenever I could go. So I called him to let him know I'd be there today. It was sudden like."

"Oh." Claire didn't know what else to say. She was happy for Belinda. But why didn't she talk about them exchanging phone numbers and possibly meeting? Weren't they supposed to share their new experiences? Especially since she was now a part of the family?

"You had a date." She stopped walking.

Blotches of rosy red bloomed on Belinda's neck and face.

She would not, could not be upset. Instead she teased. "Someone's in love."

"I don't know about looovvve. But I sure do like Drew." She kicked a pebble into the ditch. "I put on some of Grandma's foundation to cover the scars. I didn't do as good of a job as Lizbeth. But he didn't seem to notice."

"That's great." She truly meant it. "Where is he now?"

"He's goin' to Cavern Junction with his brother. He's a senior and drives. They're on their way to get burgers, fries, and malts."

"His brother was with you?"

"Nah." She began walking again. "He stayed in the car listenin' to his radio."

"Why does Drew take the bus if his brother drives to school?"

"Welp." Belinda kicked another rock with her shoe. "I asked him that, and he said his brother goes early to the library and works on an extra class so he will graduate next year."

"Kaye doesn't have a chance with Drew now."

"Not even the slightest." She pumped her arms in the air. "I can see in his eyes he likes me."

She smiled. Belinda deserved happiness. Her daddy died in a drowning accident. Her mother, Grandma Neecy's daughter, ran off to Hollywood. Claire had thought she had problems. A vehicle slowed and pulled over to the road's shoulder in front of them. She nudged her. "I don't believe it."

She squinted at the car. "Who is that?"

"The Lavender Girls."

Wendy stuck her head out of the backseat window. She waved. They hurried to meet her. "Hi." Her smile reached her eyes. "Fancy meeting you here."

Claire grinned. "What are the chances?"

"Slim to none. Of course this is not the big city, is it?"

She wanted to act kind so she spoke to the bully. "Hi, Kaye." She kept her face turned and ignored them. Someone had a chip on her shoulder. She peered into the open window of the front passenger's seat. "Hi, Mr. Tyner. I'm Claire Monteiro. My dad, Pete, works for you."

He didn't seem to recognize Claire's dad's name. She didn't mind. He tipped his hat to her. "Good to meet you, young lady."

If for no other reason, she wanted to set a good example to show Kaye. Good manners and forgiveness were always best. She herself needed to learn this better although it was the hard way. "This is my friend, Belinda Cruz."

He tipped his hat again. "Glad to meet you."

"You, too, sir."

"We best go." Mr. Tyner danced his index finger on the steering wheel. "I'm taking these girls to the movies."

Wendy waved goodbye. As the car pulled onto the highway, the two friends waved back. Kaye glared through the rear window.

"We're never going to win her over, are we, Belinda? With Wendy, I see progress. Not her."

"You know what we should do?"

"What?"

"Yahoo." Belinda reached her arms toward the sky and leaned back her head. "Why didn't I think of this before? I know how to bug her and help her at the same time."

A breeze mussed Claire's hair. "How?" She tucked the strands behind her ear.

"There's a verse in the Bible Grandma really likes. It says something like this. 'Be kind to your enemies and ya will heap coals of fire upon their heads.'"

"Never heard of it. But it's the best solution you've ever had in dealing with Kaye."

"It's sure not my idea. Thank Grandma. No, wait." She waved her hands. "Thank the Lord for writing about it to help us."

As the two friends drew closer to the store, they crossed the road. At the mention of the Bible verse, Claire had questions.

How would they heap coals of fire on Kaye? What kind act would take her by surprise?

Her biggest concern? What if it backfired and she hated them even more?

~∧~∧~

Claire flipped her pillow from under her head and smashed it into her face. She could no longer stand Grandmother Walker's snoring. Tomorrow, she would ask if she could sleep on the sofa in the caboose.

Even though it was more like a loveseat-style, it didn't matter with her height. If not the caboose, she'd set up Daddy's tent and sleep in the backyard. She'd do anything rather than listen to toe-curling snores.

She sat upright in the sleeping bag. The out of doors would be better now even though it had grown colder at night. She left the sofa and dug through a box of ratty blankets on the back porch. An old wool Army blanket could be her mattress and a thicker quilt for a topper over her sleeping bag.

She set up on a patch of grass in the backyard. She was safe from wild critters if she slept within the tall cedar fence with the gate latched. The back porch door was five feet from her ground bed. No fears. No worries.

She snuggled deeper into Daddy's sleeping bag and shut off the flashlight. She drifted to sleep, listening to coyotes yip, yipping on their mountain.

28

The backyard gate squeaked, and the porch door opened and closed. One eye opened and revealed a dark-soon-to-dawn, and she sank lower into the bag. The next time she woke, a snuffle and a spiky, moist nose tickled her ear. She yelped and then peered into golden brown eyes. Laddie dog.

As she giggled, Laddie licked her cheek with his tongue. She covered her head with her hands. "Don't." He plopped on his back next to her and wiggled closer. "No belly rubs. It's too early."

"No, it's not." Belinda peered over her head. "What in heaven's name are ya doin' out here?"

"I left the snorer." Even to her the reply sounded muffled.

"I'll ask Grandma today if ya can sleep in the caboose."

She unmasked her face from the blanket, rubbed sleep from her eyes, and she yawned. "All I need is your sofa." She pushed herself up. "We need to get ready for school."

"Yeah, ya do." Belinda straightened. "Grandma's got the cream of wheat ready, and the boys already ate."

"You go on." She folded blankets and rolled up the sleeping bag. "I'll be right there." She shivered all the way to the house, her toes damp from the grass. She dressed and washed her face. Her teeth finally stopped clicking, though goose bumps still pricked her skin. Claire hugged herself at the table and waited for Grandma Neecy to serve her food.

The older woman set a warm bowl of cereal in front of her. "Feels as though it'll freeze soon, don't ya know." She set a large plate of buttered whole wheat biscuits in the center of the table.

On their way out for chicken chores, the boys grabbed a biscuit. "Thank you, Grandma." Grayson stopped, turned, and hugged Grandma Neecy around the middle.

After they left, she frowned down at Claire. "Youngin', ya look sleep deprived."

"I feel it." She silently prayed the blessing and scooped a mouthful of cereal.

Belinda watched her eat.

"What?" Claire swiped at her chin. "Did I drip?"

"No. I think ya forgot what today is, what with ya wearing your hair in a pony tail and an old blouse."

"Today?"

"School pictures."

"Is that why you have a yellow ribbon in your hair and you're wearing your yellow dress?"

"Yep. Ya better hurry and fix yourself up."

"Oh, no." Grandma Neecy shook her head. "You'll be late."

She forgot about her food and raced to her room where she had to knock on her own door to get a nice dress off the hanger.

Grandmother Walker would be livid.

~∧~∧~

Perspiration dampened the underarms of her bright-red plaid dress as she ran to catch the bus. She grumbled the whole way. "I'll be so glad when that old woman is gone or in the apartment."

"Sorry, little buddy. I don't think we'd have room for your clothes in the caboose but at least you're sleeping with us now."

"Thank heavens." She yawned. Her brush and several bobby pins shook inside her coat pocket as her feet sprinted.

Once on the bus, Belinda brushed Claire's hair. "Drew's in the very back."

"Ouch." She swiped at the brush. "You're too rough."

"You're a tender head." She *tsk*ed and then her brush strokes stilled.

"Hi, Belinda." Drew must have moved closer by a few seats.

She twisted. His expression had a gentle feel as he watched her best friend. Smitten. Definitely.

Blushing to a near purple, Belinda folded her hands in her lap. She still held the brush. "Ah, hi Drew." She gave him a sideways glance.

It seemed to Claire that he relaxed. "I'm glad we met at the store."

Belinda nibbled on her bottom lip.

"And Claire, I had fun at your party."

Even though she still needed to style her hair, she made a decision. She stood in front of her seat. "Let's switch places, Drew.

"Sure." His grin widened to full-blown, and he jumped to his feet. Belinda scooted toward the window.

She held out a palm for the brush. "I'll finish my hair." Settled into the seat, she finished the brush strokes until there were no more tangles. She swept the side of her hair away from her ear and stuck in a bobby pin. She repeated the style on the other side. As she worked, she focused on the nearby chatter.

"Don't be so sure."

"The Lavender Girls—"

Her ears perked.

"They're from a big city."

Someone else said, "Really?"

"The one girl, Kaye is it? She's . . . expose . . . secret."

She leaned her head back to hear even better.

"It has something to do with—"

"The Monteiro's?"

She grew light headed. Kaye wouldn't. It didn't make sense. How could she tell about what Mama did without exposing herself?

Unless.

Kaye lied.

She lowered her gaze to her lap, where her knuckles grew white around her hair brush. As tears burned the bridge of her nose, she prayed. *Please, Lord, anything but this.*

No one here knew about Mama's breakdown back in Gallagher Springs. But the school audience there knew something was not right when Mama came to the awards ceremony. She even embarrassed Claire.

She readjusted a bobby pin and planned how to heap coals of fire on Kaye. But not the way Grandma Neecy meant. How do you fight against revenge? She had to stop her before it was too late.

~∧~∧~

In the hallway at school and inside the classroom, Claire dared not look anyone in the eyes. What if Kaye had already spread the rumor about Mama? Her nerves rattled in her stomach. She did not like the crowds at school after she overheard what Kaye had planned. She longed to tell the office secretary to call Grandma Neecy to pick her up. But she feared one of the students in charge of the office phone would then question her about why she needed to leave.

She already had a hard enough time avoiding Belinda's questions about why she was so quiet.

So she would stay and find a solution to stop Kaye Tyner. If it wasn't too late.

But her mind grew muddled.

At first break, she wandered to the nurse's room. It had a narrow cot, one chair, and a desk. Files stood along the wall behind the desk. She stepped inside the open door. Her shoulders stooped as though bully Kaye had won. The cot called to her. Would it be okay to lie down without permission?

Maybe with a bit of quiet, she could figure how to save Mama's reputation.

She pulled off her shoes, stretched on the cot, and covered her knees with the skirt of her dress. Her homeroom class was first to take their student photos. She had tried to smile for the photographer. Her heart forgot how.

Jumbled feelings swept through her. *Why is life so hard?* Why were there problems like Mama's? One which had threatened to split their family once before? She was going to be okay with Grandma Neecy here, but now there was Grandmother Walker along with the Lavender Girls.

A niggle pecked at her dismal brain, something about a jar.

She had no blessing to offer the Blessing Jar.

The bell rang and startled Claire from her dozing. A sad longing overwhelmed her. She began to weep and stifled her cries into the starched pillow. If Mama knew, she would depend on her to stop this horrid rumor. If she didn't, her mother might go into a deep depression.

"May I help you?" Gentle fingers touched her forehead.

She peered into the face of Miss Rose. She kneeled next to the cot. "Claire?" She reached for something near the cot, and came back with a handful of tissue. She dabbed at her cheeks. "Even if you don't feel like talking, at least nod or shake your head."

At the kind words, she blubbered like a baby.

"Do you hurt somewhere?"

She shook her head no. *My heart.*

"Are you ill?"

No again. *Sick to my stomach.*

Miss Rose's doe eyes seemed to survey Claire's face. "Problems?"

She nodded yes and shut her lids again. *Always.*

"Maybe at lunch break, we can eat our lunch here at this desk."

From the creak of the floor boards and Miss Rose taking her warmth with her, she opened her eyes. Miss Rose smiled. "I'll let the office know you're unable to attend the next two classes. Is that okay?"

Her throat had gone dry as dust and she blinked.

She touched Claire's forehead. "I'll see you then." She readjusted her thick, black glasses on her nose. "Problems have a way of making us need extra rest." She nodded and left the room.

Miss Rose had no way of knowing a small part of her problem was lack of sleep. When was the last time she'd slept without waking? Sometime before Grandmother Walker came and snored the night through.

She reached under the cot for the blanket she had seen earlier and covered herself to her chin. She relaxed, and she gave in to her exhaustion and fell asleep.

Someone tapped her shoulder, and she startled.

Though Miss Rose didn't smile, her eyes were soft and kind. Trustful. "Feel any better, Claire?"

She sat upright. "I don't have my lunch."

"I'll share mine." She placed a medium-sized sack on the desk. "I always bring extra. A habit from when Mama packed my school lunches with too much food." She reached into the bag and brought out a large whole wheat sandwich split in half. She directed it at Claire. "I hope you like turkey."

She took the half offered to her. "Did you bake this bread?" She laid the sandwich on the napkin in front of her.

"Yes." She smiled. "I've been experimenting with different flours, and making round loaves of European style bread."

She could smell the wheat aroma. "Hmmm. This smells good." Her belly growled.

"Oops." She covered her mouth. "You're hungry."

Was she supposed to say excuse me for the growl which erupted in her stomach? She had learned in Miss Rose's class she had strict codes of conduct. She didn't want to offend her.

Claire was about to pray in silence and thank God for the food, but Miss Rose said, "May I say the blessing?"

She bowed her head to the question.

"Thank you, Father, for this food we're about to eat. Please help Claire in whatever is troubling her. In Jesus' name. Amen."

She breathed her amen, folded her hands on the desk, and waited for Miss Rose to pick up her half of the sandwich.

As they both ate, comfortable silence filled the tiny room. After finishing the sandwich, Miss Rose handed her two oatmeal cookies with flakes of coconut. "No, thank you. I don't care for coconut."

After a bit, refreshed and full, she decided to trust Miss Rose. She placed her arms on the desk and leaned forward. "My mama almost died last year while she gave birth to my brother."

The line deepened at the soft wrinkle on Miss Rose's forehead.

"Almost dying changed Mama. Everyone in our family was hurt by her." She inhaled. "This is between us?"

"Of course."

"Okay. There's this girl in school. One of the two you said I should invite to Belinda's birthday party weeks ago. Do you remember?"

Her expression stiffened. "Kaye Tyner?"

Of course Miss Rose knew her. She taught Kaye in PE class. "When I was on the bus this morning, some girls talked. They said Kaye knows a secret about my family. That she's going to tell the whole school."

"That is cruel."

"This is a secret I thought was left behind in Gallagher Springs where I went to school last year." She nibbled on her ragged fingernail.

"How does Kaye know about your mama?" Her mouth pursed in a thin line. "Or rather, what does she know about your mama?"

"We went to the same school. Her dad is one of the bosses for the tunnels they put in around the country."

"Ah, ha. Like the Gaskey tunnel job here." She lowered her gaze and picked at crumbs on her napkin. "I don't even want to know what secret it is you're guarding. That part is unnecessary."

"Thank you. I have to protect my mother." She drew a deep breath. "I thought if I came in here where it was quiet, I would figure out a plan."

She folded her hands on the desk. "We need to stop Kaye from spreading private information that would only hurt others."

"What should I do, Miss Rose?"

Her eyes gleamed. Was that mischief in Claire's very proper teacher's eyes? She angled her head. "I think I may be able to help."

Tingles spread throughout her limbs.

She seemed to search Claire's face. "Why don't I involve the principal? You could tell him your situation. But you would have to tell him what happened with your mama so he can judge whether or not to call Kaye into his office. I know our principal would never expose your family secret. He also would forbid her from spreading rumors or threaten to expel her from school if the situation called for it."

"I need to talk to him right now. If I know Kaye, it may be too late."

"I hadn't thought of that." Miss Rose's face sagged.

"Will you go with me to the principal's office?"

29

In Principal Meyers's outer office, she waited in a chair. She had asked Miss Rose to stay with her, but she believed it best for Claire to have fewer people involved.

She wasn't so sure Miss Rose had the right idea. Nibble, nibble, nibble. Her fingernail was way too short. The next nibble would draw blood. She fisted her fingers in her lap.

Students walked by, and she longed to catch a glimpse of her best friend. She'd come in and sit with her. Every few minutes, she spoke the same words to God in a silent prayer. "Lord, please keep Kaye's mouth shut."

After an eternity, Principal Meyer's door opened. A slump-shouldered eighth grade boy hurried toward the open doorway. He shrugged at her on his way out.

The principal was a much taller man than her daddy. He waved her in, and she followed him to his desk. "Have a seat."

Her legs shook. But she didn't miss the chair, fall on the floor, and make herself look like an idiot.

He sat also and placed his clasped hands in front of him on the desk. "How can I help you, Claire?"

She began the story with what Mama did at the awards ceremony in Gallagher Springs, what Kaye said to make it worse, and she finished her story with a flinch. "This morning, I overheard a student say Kaye's going to tell kids a secret about my family."

His eyes narrowed. He drummed his fingers on his desk. "Well, Claire." He sat back in his chair, and crossed his arms over his chest. "I'm sorry you and your family have had a hard time. And I'll do all I can to stop this nonsense." He sat forward again. "You know Kaye may deny this plan she has if she hasn't already spread the gossip."

"I understand, but at least she'll be stopped. That's all I want." She stuck another fingernail between her teeth, but then allowed her hand to fall in her lap.

They both stood. "Thank you, sir, for your help."

As she headed for the door, the principal spoke. "If she has already spread the rumor, I'll see to it she is disciplined."

Claire nodded, opened the door, and stepped into the hall. She went a few paces before she stopped. There at the secretary's desk sat Kaye. She was on the phone and scribbled on paper. Her boy-cut brown hair bobbed as she spoke.

Legs frozen to the floor, she wondered if she should go back into the principal's waiting area until the bell rang. Or should she hurry past Kaye and act like she didn't have a twenty minute conversation with Principal Meyers? Her feet swiveled. And she bumped into his chest.

He grabbed Claire before she hit the floor. "Hey there." He chuckled. "Did you forget something?"

Behind her in the secretary's office, Kaye said, "Today at two o'clock? Okay, I'm taking the message. Thank you for calling. What? My name? Kaye Tyner. Yes. Goodbye."

Claire kept her eyes on the principal. His nose twitched. "Would you like to take over for Miss Tyner until Mrs. Preston returns?" He nudged her toward the secretary's office as Claire's steps faltered.

Kaye's jaw went slack. She closed it just as fast and beamed a fake smile. "Hi, Claire. May I help you?" She glanced at Principal Meyers.

He crooked his index finger for her to follow him and entered his office.

Her face masked over and as Claire was about to pass her, Kaye said, "If I were you, I'd be real careful whose name you bash."

She remained calm. Only sorrow washed over her for how things had gotten out of control. So far she had almost always kept her word to Grandma Neecy about being more kind, though it had been hard. All she wanted now was to keep her mama's name from being tainted.

"I'm not you, Kaye. I wouldn't spread gossip about anyone, even if it were true. And especially if it hurt an entire family." She shrugged. "I'd be too ashamed. But I *will* protect my family. So I told the truth to the one the person who can stop you."

Principal Meyers appeared in his doorway. "Are you coming, Miss Tyner?"

Kaye took a backward step from Claire. Her eyes flicked this way and that. "What have you done to me?"

He snapped his fingers and waved for her to follow him.

The secretary's phone rang. She hurried to the desk and grabbed the receiver. She scribbled the message. When the call ended, she rewrote the note in neater print on a clean sheet.

"Hey, little buddy, there ya are." Belinda leaned against the counter in the hall. Her grin spread wide as the Illinois River near her house. "I've been lookin' all over for ya." She scratched at her neck.

She moved to lean against the counter and wanted to hug her dear friend to help wash away Kaye's mean words. "You will never believe this day." She squeezed her arm. "I'm so glad to see you."

She waved a hand at the office. "You've stepped up in the world, Miss segritary."

She didn't have the heart to correct her misuse of secretary. "I'm just taking Kaye's place for a few minutes."

"What?" Belinda squinted.

"I can't explain. Kaye's in the principal's office."

She slammed a palm on the counter. "Get out of town." All humor left her expression. "You're killin' me with curiosity."

The principal's voice drew near. She shooed Belinda with a flick of her fingers and plopped into the secretary's chair. Kaye's face was smudged with red blotches, her lashes wet. Claire wanted to stare, but she didn't, and she never thought anything could make Kaye Tyner cry.

Principal Meyer gripped her shoulder. "Go back to work."

Claire moved toward the door, ready to retreat to the safety of her friend. She peeked at Kaye as they passed. Whatever he said, it had made a hefty impression. She would not raise her head, and she sniffled into a tissue.

Relief washed over her like a warm blanket on a frigid night.

~~^~~

She fast-walked down the hall and met Belinda where she stood only yards from the office. The little sneak hadn't gone far. She grabbed Claire's arm. "Tell me everything before the bell rings."

"Let me catch my breath."

"I know a place we can talk." And she grabbed her by the wrist. As they entered the gym, she guided them toward the last set of bleachers. They went underneath, sat on the floor, and faced each other.

Belinda slapped a hand on the wall. "I want to hear every stinkin' detail."

Sitting cross-legged, she hurried her words. "It started on the bus this morning." She told her about the conversation she'd overheard on the bus. How she felt so sick to her stomach, she laid down on the cot in the nurse's room. How once there, she hoped to find a solution.

"Whoa the horses. That Kaye Tyner is a piece of work and has a soul as dried as a shriveled mushroom."

She couldn't agree more and continued her story, ending with the visit to the principal's office.

"But she's not going to tell what happened to your mama because of the principal?"

"I don't know." She pulled her knees to her chest and rested her cheek there. "I'm so tired." She told Belinda about how upset Kaye was after her visit with Principal Meyers. "So because she was allowed back to the secretary's office, I'm thinking she hadn't gossiped."

"I can't believe Kaye cried." Belinda retied the strings on her shoes. "That has to be good, right? That she didn't get expelled so she hadn't told anyone."

The bell rang. It was so loud in the gym she covered her ears with her hands. As they left, Claire hoped Principal Meyers was true to his word. That he would have disciplined Kaye if necessary.

At their lockers near the gym doors, Claire said hi to several girls as they past. She tested them to see if they knew because their expressions would tell her everything.

Lizbeth popped over to talk to them after she got her books. "Hey, I saw you in the secretary's office, Miss Claire." She grinned.

She didn't act nervous or anything, like she would be if she had heard a horrible thing about Mama. Claire heaved a sigh of relief. Mama's secret was safe. "I filled in is all."

The three friends got in step together to attend the next class.

~∧~∧~

Home dear home. She grew excited for evening chores, family time around the dining room table. Except for

239

mornings, this is where they took their meals because there were so many of them. And she couldn't wait to drop a pine cone or two into the Blessing Jar.

The only question Claire could not shake was a difficult one. How would anyone, even Grandma Neecy, expect her to show Kaye kindness now? All she wanted was to avoid the mean girl. She didn't care about heaping coals of fire upon Kaye to help save her soul.

As Belinda and Drew visited in the bus seat in front of her, she wondered on heaping coals from the Bible. She decided to read about it for herself. If she did, maybe, just maybe she'd come to terms with being kind to the meanest bully.

"Wake up, sleeping beauty." Belinda tugged on her sleeve. "It's our stop."

She didn't even know she had fallen asleep, but slowly gathered her few books and stood. She swayed in the isle, still tired from her too-short nap. How many naps did that make in one day? Three? Emotional upheavals exhausted her to the core.

When Claire stepped from the bus a cold wind wrapped around her like a sheet of ice. She shivered in her light-weight jacket. "Feels like snow."

Belinda walked beside her on the long driveway. "Already?"

"Yes, I can tell." Instead of going to the front door, she grabbed Belinda's hand and told her to follow.

"Where we going?"

"The caboose. I have to read that scripture Grandma Neecy talked about."

"Ya mean the one where ya heap coals of fire on someone by being nice to them?"

"Yes." She waited for Belinda to go in first and hoped Grandma Neecy was inside.

She met them at the door. "I was just leavin', 'cause I knew ya youngins was comin'." A bit of chocolate was smeared at the corner of her mouth.

The girls hugged her. "Before you go, would you show me the verse about heaping coals of fire on someone's head?"

Her wrinkles wrinkled deeper. "Well, sure." She stepped back inside and opened her Bible. It took only a moment before she tapped a finger on the page. The girls leaned in. "It reads here like this, 'Therefore if thine enemy hunger, feed him; if he thirst, give him drink: for in so doing thou shalt heap coals of fire on his head.'" She gazed at first one and then the other of the two girls.

"But Kaye's not in need of drink or food. She's rich."

Everyone grew silent. Grandma Neecy stared at her Bible. "Well then, how about these two verses above that one. It reads, 'If it be possible, as much as lieth in you, live peaceably with all men. Dearly beloved, avenge not yourselves, but rather give place unto wrath: for it is written, Vengeance is mine; I will repay, saith the Lord.'" She tapped the page. "Those three verses are in Roman 12:18 through 20." She raised a finger. "There's one more verse to sum it all up and that's 21. "Be not overcome of evil, but overcome evil with good."

"Can you explain this to me?" Claire peered over the page at the verses.

"Sure, darlin'. What it means in simple words is to live as peaceful as ya can with others. And it is not yer place to get someone back who has been mean."

"That's what I'm trying to do with Kaye."

Grandma Neecy tapped Belinda on the shoulder. "How are ya doin' with that?"

"Not so good, Grandma."

She placed the Bible on the table and moved past them. "I've got to get back in there. The boys will be sniffin' out a snack."

When she left, Claire plopped on the sofa. "So. Kaye doesn't need food or water. And God wants us as peaceful with her as earthly possible."

"Yep." She placed her empty sack lunch on the tiny kitchen counter. "I gotta stop wantin' revenge. I'm sinnin'." She slumped. "I don't know if I can." Her eyes seemed to plead for help.

"Really, it's not our battle. It sounds like it's between God and Kaye. If we act right, that's got to show her a different way. Correct?"

"I suppose." She shot upright. "I know. How about we put a pine cone in the Blessing Jar in the mornings before we go to school? Ya know, thinkin' positive to begin our day."

"That will help. We also need to pray more. Together we'll pray every day for God to help us not care so much about what she does."

The friends shook on it, and then hooked their little fingers together and both said, "Pinky promise."

Could they both be kinder no matter what happens?

30

"My daughter has no need to stay in a foreign state. She should be here, and what am I to do alone this winter?"

Grandmother Walker.

Did this mean what she thought it meant?

With the Bible verses still fresh on her mind, she and Belinda were determined to weather the problems with Kaye Tyner. Now she must use those same Scriptures on an old lady she never wanted here in the first place.

Grandmother Walker sat at the table and waved a letter, while Mama sat at the table feeding applesauce to Feather in his highchair. Her good leg bounced in a rhythm below the table, her other was propped on an empty stool.

Feather giggled and chattered, and the cheer he voiced was almost drowned out by Grandmother Walker's rants.

She dared to interrupt so she could kiss her mother's cheek. "Hi, Mama." She drew an arm around her. Did the old woman drill holes on her back as she chattered back and forth with the baby? After today, she did not care.

"Well?" She flapped the one page letter in the air again. "What are you going to do about this, Dotty?"

In response it seemed, Mama's top teeth covered her bottom lip. Why wasn't she saying anything? Claire resented that she always jumped when Grandmother Walker spoke.

She had spent the day in defense of her mother. Why not finish the day doing the same? Go for the highest prize. She faced the cranky old woman. "Grandmother Walker?"

"You, young lady, are barging into an adult conversation."

Did her expression waver between a scold and fear? That's right. Grandmother Walker's tobacco chew that she wanted Claire to keep secret. "But Mama can't fix your problem." She hated to say the next part because it was more of a lie. Was this her part in an act of kindness? Would the lie turn to truth if she practiced to mean what she said? Besides, she quoted Daddy. "You have a place here as long as you need." She gulped on the last word. Anything for Mama.

"But I want to go home."

The corners of Mama's mouth lifted. "Yes, of course you do." Her knee stilled. Her white knuckles regained color as she released the strangle hold on Feather's spoon of applesauce.

Claire's insides settled as the soft lines of Mama's face eased. She slapped her thighs and changed the subject. "Let's get a snack, Belinda."

Her brothers sat with a large peanut butter cookie each in their hands. As her vision landed on them, she almost chuckled and turned away. She recalled how their heads ping ponged between her and Grandmother Walker while they spoke.

As she chose two glasses from the cupboard, Belinda cupped her hand around her ear. "Ya put out her little forest fire." She snickered.

"I was nice about it, wasn't I?"

Belinda brought milk from the refrigerator and poured it into the glasses. "You did that real—"

"Wait a doggone minute. What about sleeping arrangements?" The old lady snorted.

Claire hesitated and then . . . "Daddy says he's still working on the little room connected to his shop. You'll be able to stay in your own little house soon, Grandmother Walker." She truly believed she would be pleased.

But her face swelled. Her complexion bloomed as purple as a shooting star flower which sprouted each spring. "You'd toss me out? Treat me like some common criminal?"

Mama paled and Claire clamped her mouth. She brought her glass of milk and cookie to the table, and she and Belinda ate and drank and chatted.

Later before bed, the two friends dropped their pine cones in the Blessing Jar. She was grateful she stopped Kaye before she hurt Mama. Belinda said she was blessed Drew still acted like he cared about her.

~∧~∧~

The friends agreed to keep each other from saying anything other than kind words to Kaye. They said hi to the Lavender Girls as they passed them in the hall. They sat next to them during lunch. Wendy chatted, but Kaye stayed quiet, solemn. Whenever Claire spoke to Kaye, her eyes darted.

The BGs gathered at their log by their tree and talked about Kaye.

Lizbeth picked at her chipped fingernail polish. "Well, I believe she realizes she can't treat people like she does."

She glanced at her other friend. "Maybe."

"My mother says I can have a sleepover before the baby's born."

"When?" Claire perked up at the idea.

"I thought not this weekend but next. I can invite five girls to make six altogether. Won't that be fun? We can stay in the basement where it's set up like a studio apartment."

She clapped. "It sounds fun."

"Who will ya invite?"

"Lorene and you two. That's four of us. And to be a good example? The Lavender Girls."

Belinda stiffened. "I don't—"

"I think it's a good idea." She touched her hand. "It'll be our time to show Kaye we forgive her. We want her to see Jesus in us like Grandma Neecy said."

But Belinda's face bunched into a knot.

She smiled. "Right?"

After several long moments, she nodded. "Who's goin' to invite them, 'cause it won't be me."

"That's my job." Lizbeth stood.

"Alrighty." She shivered as a gust of wind blew. "Do you need us to come along?"

"Well." She batted her lashes. "I could use the support. Kaye intimidates me."

"But you're invitin' them?"

"It's the right thing to do."

"They're comin'."

"Okay. Here I go."

Claire figured this could go one of two ways, because she was sure they wouldn't expect this.

The Lavender Girls stopped in front of them.

"I'm glad you're here."

"Oh?" Wendy tilted her head. "Why is that?"

Kaye wore a blank expression and her eyes appeared to follow Lizbeth's gestures.

"It just so happens I'm allowed to host a slumber party at my house not this weekend but next." She bent forward a bit. "You're both invited."

Kaye straightened her shoulders. "Why?"

"Thank you for thinking of us."

"Well? Do you want to come?"

"Yes. We'd like to have you both." Claire stared up at her best friend. "Right?"

"Sure." She crossed her arms, but dropped them to her sides.

The bell rang. The Lavender Girls went ahead of the Better Girls Club. Claire kept in step with her friends. "That went well, but I'm a bit worried. One second Kaye's like a statue, the next she's ready for a verbal fight."

"I think my slumber party will warm her cold heart. Wendy is friendlier. Now it's her turn."

"Don't hold your breath." Belinda snorted. "I would never let down my guard around her. Or even away from her."

"Ah, come on," Lizbeth waved a hand, "I think there's a good spot in everyone's heart. Some have less than others. Some need to find it."

Claire prayed so for all their sakes.

The girls arrived at the back double doors that led to the hall. Belinda gripped the handle of the door. "We'll see about that on slumber party night."

Yes they would.

~^~^~

The girls were ready to drop their pine cones in the Blessings Jar. Claire went first. "I'm blessed because I'm now sleeping in the caboose." She let her cone fall. She flashed Belinda a wide grin. "Your turn."

Her cone hovered over the jar. "I feel blessed 'cause Claire gets to bunk with me from now on." Her fingers let go and the cone fell.

"That was so sweet."

She lifted the jar. "It's true." She placed it on the shelf in the kitchen near the table. "Grandma and I fixed an area for ya. The sofa is now yours."

Everyone else had gone to bed, so the two friends turned off the kitchen lights. As they pushed open the pantry door, a series of snorts and snores echoed from the direction of Claire's room.

Both girls froze. Claire slapped her forehead with the pad of her hand. "There she goes again. Doesn't she sound like a chain saw with a hiccup?"

"Sure enough."

"Let's go." She shoved through the pantry door. "I'm so grateful I don't have to hear her anymore. At least while she sleeps."

"Oh, but." She put out a hand to stop her. "Grandma snores too, just nothin' like lumber Jane sawing on a log."

"Then I'll live."

31

She forgot to watch the clock while she stuffed a small bag full of clothes for the slumber party.

The girls chose a seat toward the middle. She heaved a sigh of relief. They had almost missed the bus.

"Hey, Drew's not here today."

"Oh?" She spread her skirt over her knees. "I didn't notice."

"Do ya think ya got everything for the slumber party?"

"I do. I sure hope we have a good time."

"Yeah." Belinda blew out a breath like she'd been holding it. "Ya never know with the Lavender Girls."

That was the truth. While she was eager for the event, part of her was filled with dread. "I believe my head is in a bubble."

"What do ya mean?"

"Since when have the Lavender Girls never caused a problem? Well, lately, Wendy hasn't."

"She seems a little sad, but nice."

"If I tell you something, you have to keep it a secret."

"Oookay."

"Her mom left the family."

"Just like mine."

"I'm sorry." She lowered her gaze. "That probably stirs up bad feelings."

"Nah. No worries, little buddy. I really don't miss my ma like I once did." She sniffed.

"You do too. I'm so thoughtless." She pierced her with a look.

"No, little buddy. I'm really not sad. Grandma Neecy loves me and takes good care of me. I'm happy." She lowered her lashes. "My ma stirred more trouble than a skunk in a barnyard. Life's easier without her."

"If you're sure." Belinda always said what she meant, so this made her relax.

Now, if she would not fret over what the Lavender Girls might do at the slumber party.

~∧~∧~

The school morning crept like a baby learning to crawl.

She suffered nervous jitters. Excited one moment. The next, fearful they were headed for disaster. She wasn't worried about Wendy. But Kaye Tyner billowed like a storm cloud ready to bluster and flash lightning. Deep in her belly, she had no doubt there would be trouble. She wanted to talk to Belinda about it. See if they could form a plan of how to respond.

The BGs huddled on a lunch bench Claire had chosen in a remote part of the cafeteria.

"What's this about?" Lizbeth unpacked her sack lunch. "Has something happened? With, you know."

She sat in the middle, so both her friends could hear her low voice. "Before I tell you, I wanted to make sure you both are willing to add Lorene to our club."

Both girls said yes.

"Good. I've got a bad feeling."

"Uh-oh." Belinda bit into her tuna sandwich. "Ya know about Claire's bad feelin's, right?"

"She's mentioned it a time or two. Is this about our two guests coming tonight?"

"Yes. We need a plan. To expect the worst and hope for the best."

"Okay," they both said.

"This way, we're not shocked or upset. We have to act as brave as lions."

"Should I warn my mom and get her support?"

"Great idea. Just like I told Daddy and Grandma Neecy we could have trouble with them at both our parties."

"And if ya want to kick 'em out of your house, I'd do the job."

"We haven't made a plan, and they're coming this way," Lizbeth whispered.

She moaned.

The Lavender Girls placed their hot lunch trays on the table across from the BGs. They each said hi but otherwise ate their lunch. Halfway through her sandwich, Claire's tuna was beginning to rise toward her throat. Did they guess the BGs were talking about them? Is that why they came clear across the cafeteria to sit with them?

Surely not.

"So." Kaye's eyes became mere slits. "What were you girls jabbering about?"

Lizbeth choked on her drink and sprayed grape juice onto Wendy's plate. Belinda patted her on the back.

"That's so disgusting." Kaye moved a few inches away.

Wendy gave her a sideways glance. "I'm going to have to get a new tray of food."

"I'm so sorry." She swiped at the juice on her chin and between them on the table.

"I'll get a wet rag from the cook." Wendy lifted her tray and headed back to the food line.

"I think you were talking about us. And you did that on purpose, Lizbeth."

Claire helped her mop the mess with her already soggy napkin. She inhaled and leaned back as though ready to run. My poor sweet friend.

"There better not be any spit in this."

"Oh, stop, Tyner." Belinda glared. "Ya are so melodramatic."

Claire pressed on her mouth to hide a grin. Her friend's use of words had grown bigger this year, and she got that one correct.

"What's so funny, *ClaireLee*?" Kaye forked into her mashed potatoes and gravy.

"I'm not—"

"What Claire's trying to say is," Belinda placed her palms on the table, "don't put her two names together.

Never. That is an old rule ya continue to break." She sliced a hand through the air. "No more. Got it?"

Kaye stared at her food and ate the entire time Belinda spoke. She laid down her fork and buttered her roll. "Stupid rule."

Lizbeth grabbed Claire's hand under the table and squeezed. Belinda stood. She sauntered around the table and stopped behind Kaye. Quick as a wink, she scooped a handful of Kaye's mashed potatoes and gravy. Kaye gasped. Her face tilted. Belinda plopped the food on her head and smeared it around with a "gotcha!" smile.

"Oh, have mercy." Lizbeth pressed her mouth with her fist.

Claire nibbled her bottom lip. *She's gone and done it now.*

The bully shot up from the bench and threw a handful of green beans.

Belinda dodged the vegetables mostly, but one stuck in her hair. She giggled. "Ya missed me, ya missed me, now ya gotta—"

"You are such a backward hillbilly hick, scar—"

"What's going on?" Wendy rushed to Kaye's side.

"She ruined my hair."

"You started this, Belinda?"

"No. I did not." She walked back to her side of the table. "I swear to ya, Wendy, if ya don't do something about her, I will. This is just the start of how mad I can get."

Wendy set her tray down and handed a wet cloth to Lizbeth. "What did she do?"

Kids gathered near their table. Some giggled. Some cheered. *Oh, dear, this is bad.* They weren't even at the slumber party and trouble had already started.

"What's the meaning of this?"

Miss Rose.

Her eyes wandered along the table, over the girls, and settled on Kaye. "Is that potatoes and gravy in your hair?"

"Belinda did it. She's always after me."

"Belinda?" Miss Rose lifted her glasses higher on the bridge of her nose. "Did you?"

She had the decency to lower her eyes. "Ahhh, I can explain."

"What happened here, Claire?"

She didn't see that one coming, and she slouched. What should she say? She didn't want to get Belinda in trouble. But she couldn't lie. She'd done enough lying in Gallagher Springs to last a lifetime. And her almost lie to Grandmother Walker was as close as she dared.

"I've told you a bit about Kaye." Miss Rose tapped her foot. "She never knows when to quit." She mustered all her emotion with one look. "When is it going to stop? She may not be a bully so much as to hurt people physically. But she is still a bully. She bullies with her threats. She bullies with her taunts."

Miss Rose stilled the tapping toes and studied her as though she had listened with her heart.

Belinda stood in front of the teacher. "I got carried away, Miss Rose, and I'm sorry."

"Well." She glanced between Belinda and Kaye. "This *is* complicated."

"It is." Claire moved off the bench. "Very complicated. But I'm afraid there's been no way to solve the problem. Believe me, we are trying." She now stood in front of Miss Rose in support of her friend. "Belinda's grandma has been talking to us. Helping us to know what to do with Kaye and her bullying. She's even helped us to understand why someone would bully."

"Don't talk about me in front of—"

"Oh, yeah. Grandma's been telling us to be like Jesus. What would Jesus expect of us? Do we have Jesus in our hearts, and all that?"

The corner of the teacher's mouth twitched.

Did she hide a smile?

"I may have an idea. Come with me girls." She scanned their faces in a serious expression once again.

The two enemies did not budge.

Miss Rose twisted to glance over her shoulder. "I said, let's go. It's either to the principal's office or to the girls' locker room in the gym."

Lizbeth frowned at Claire and her lips quivered.

The two enemies followed the teacher from the cafeteria while the other girls stared after them. What would happen next, Claire could not guess.

~^~^~

The rest of the school day passed in a blur. The three BGs shared one class together but there was no chance to talk. For all of her good intentions to make a plan during lunch, they fell by the wayside.

They would ride the bus together to Lizbeth's. Maybe then, they could figure out a plan. Or maybe the Lavender Girls would not come tonight. Especially after what Belinda did to Kaye.

At the lockers, the BGs gathered. They took what was needed for the weekend and left the locker area to meet the bus. On the way, Lorene joined them.

Claire walked between Belinda and Lorene. "We need to finish our discussion about a plan if there's trouble."

"You mean about tonight?" Lorene peered at her. "Lizbeth told me the Lavender Girls are invited. And of course the whole school knows about the food fight."

"Yes. But first, we want you in our Better Girls Club."

"Count me in." Lorene stopped walking. "Better as in better than the Lavender Girls?" All the others nodded, and Lorene smiled. "I like that."

Belinda had been too quiet. Claire waited for her to tell them what happened after she and Kaye left with Miss Rose. But with their time crunch, it was more important to make a plan for tonight. She opened her mouth. "So—"

"There's something ya should know, little buddy."

"Okay." As they walked away from the school building, she waited and listened.

"We'll talk on the bus."

Lizbeth peered at her. "Well, Belinda, that could be a problem."

Claire asked, "Why?"

"The Lavender Girls ride my bus."

"Of course they do." She slapped her forehead. "There are only two buses, and they don't ride ours."

The girls got into the bus line. It seemed to her all four of them looked for the Lavender Girls. They did not spot them anywhere. Some kids were already on the bus, so maybe they were with that crowd.

As they climbed the steps, Belinda looked back at the others. "We need to sit together in two seats."

But there was only one empty seat. Belinda wasn't accepting this. She asked a boy to move to a seat which had only one occupant. He moved. While she arranged the seating, Claire looked for Wendy and Kaye. She spotted them. No way would they hear their conversation. They were at the back of the bus with, she counted, seven rows between them.

After the bus moved forward, Belinda, who sat in the seat with Lorene, twisted to face the others. "Ya will never guess what Miss Rose had in mind." Her expression hardened. "She made me clean the potatoes and gravy from Kaye's hair in one of the locker room sinks."

"No." Claire's hand flew to her mouth.

Lizbeth stared at Belinda slack-jawed. Lorene pursed her lips over her braces.

"Yep." She twisted her mouth into a knot. "It was a most humblin' experience." She glanced at all three girls. "Have ya ever had to wash the hair of your enemy?"

Each of them shook their heads no.

"Didn't think so." Belinda shrugged. "I been thinkin'. Maybe because I didn't listen to Grandma, God had to grab hold of me and shake me. But good."

"That would humiliate me." Claire fiddled with her fingers on her lap.

"Me too." It seemed Lizbeth's eyes bore into Belinda's. "I'm so sorry."

"I saw Miss Rose leading you girls from the cafeteria." Lorene shook her head back and forth. "I put two and two together with all the mush in Kaye's hair."

"Don't be sorry, Lizbeth. I had it comin'."

"You don't hate her anymore?" Claire could hardly believe what she was hearing.

"I never said I hated her." Belinda gripped the back of the seat in front of her. "I just don't feel I can like or ever trust her. How can I after the names she called me in Gallagher Springs?"

"What kind of names?" Lizbeth frowned.

Lorene leaned closer to Belinda.

"The worse one was scar face, because it's true."

Claire squeezed her hand. "But, Belinda, remember, Kaye has a scarred heart. We don't know how it got that way. But it is, just like Grandma Neecy said. She is unhappy and miserable. And I never thanked you. You came to my defense about her spewing out my full name like dirt in her mouth."

"I overreacted." Belinda sighed. "I won't do it again. If Grandma found out what I did." She lowered her chin. "She would be so disappointed."

"Why don't we make our plan?" Lizbeth cleared her throat. "My bus stop is in a few minutes."

The BGs put their heads together and created one. They liked what they decided. They had become a strong force.

32

All six girls stepped off the school bus.

Lizbeth's mom met them with a smile, her hair in a ponytail, and an apron stretched across her baby belly. "Welcome, ladies. I've laid out snacks and a drink for each of you at the dining room table." She waved them inside.

They chattered and giggled as the group placed their belongings on the sofa. Lizbeth's mom had placed a party platter of assorted cookies in the center of the table. Their drinks were grape juice, made from grapes grown at the back of the family's property.

She rested her hands on top of her belly. "When you're finished eating, Lizbeth will show you to the basement guest room. Be sure to take your belongings. If you need anything, let me know." With that, she turned and exited the room.

Lizbeth said, "excuse me," and hurried after her mom. Claire was certain this was when she would alert her mom to possible trouble with the Lavender Girls.

She glanced at Wendy and Kaye every few minutes. The two had grown quiet. Wendy fidgeted in her seat as though she sat on a sticker, and Kaye kept her chin raised as though she were wearing a crown.

"Hey." Belinda nudged Claire's elbow. "Lizbeth says they have a pool table in the basement."

A cookie crumb clung to the side of Claire's mouth. She licked it off. "I hear it's a fun game."

Kaye slapped the table with her hand. "Don't tell me, Claire, that you've never played pool."

"I have not."

Lorene waved a hand. "I haven't either."

Lizbeth rushed back to the table and began eating. "You haven't what?"

"Lorene and Claire say they don't know how to play pool." Kaye shook her head. "Well, we'll have to teach them, won't we, Wendy?"

Belinda stood to clean her place at the table. "I know how to play."

Wendy didn't answer as she munched on her cookie.

Everyone finished and followed Lizbeth down to the basement. Claire gasped at the sight of the large, bright, and colorful room. Moss green walls, three hanging lights made from deer horns, and three double beds with floral-designed quilts. She walked around the pool table in the center of the large room. A tiny kitchen lined one wall with a sink, miniature refrigerator, stove, counters, and cupboards. Claire grew excited. "You could live down here."

Kaye crossed her arms and leaned against one wall. "This is nothing like my parents' basement."

The BGs swiveled to face her. They nodded ever so slightly. The girls were ready to use their plan to maintain a more peaceful atmosphere.

Lizbeth took a step forward. "I feel a bit hurt by your comparing your basement to mine." She touched her chest. "Although, I'm not saying mine is better than yours, because I've never seen your basement." She moved closer to Kaye. "I don't mean to complain, and I'd like to be your friend."

Her mouth gapped wide enough to stuff in an orange. "You've got to be kidding."

"Nope." She grinned. "I'm sure not." She touched Kaye's shoulder, but she shrugged and Lizbeth's hand fell away.

The room grew silent. Claire snuck a peek at Wendy.

She stared at Kaye. She glanced back at her, and Wendy gave her a subtle nod. Kaye released a long breath. "Okay, Lizbeth."

"Good."

Kaye's face flushed as though she just did the hardest thing ever.

Claire was still trying to figure out Kaye. Could it be that her mom did not forgive easily and was hard on her? Could this be why she was such a cranky person? Because the few times she had seen Kaye's dad, he acted like a kind and gentle man.

"Okay." Lizbeth clapped. "Let's play teams in a game of pool." She walked over to a row of long cue sticks attached to holders on the wall. "I think we should pair people who don't know how to play with those who do. Wendy, Belinda, and Claire you're on one team. Kaye, Lorene, and I will be on another." Each team received a stick.

The girls began the game with Lizbeth's team going first. She coached Lorene, and Belinda coached Claire. At one point, Lorene smacked a ball with the stick so hard that it bounced. It dropped on the floor. The girls giggled and exclaimed over the silly sight. All but Kaye.

She glared. "What a dumb play." She glanced at the ball underneath the pool table. "You have to keep the ball *on* the table, Lorene."

The BGs stared at Lorene.

"What?" Kaye blinked. "Did I hurt poor Lorene's feelings?"

No one spoke. Claire hoped she would understand from the last time she said an unkind thing. When she said nothing and raised her chin at them, Claire stood in front of her. "Sometimes, more often than I care to admit, I get cranky at my younger siblings. I even make my little sister cry. When that happens, I tell her I'm sorry. Lolly always forgives me."

"Well." Kaye stared at her shoes. "I, I guess I'm known to speak before I think."

"We all do, right girls?" Everyone nodded, even Wendy. "And to say we're sorry is an act of kindness and the need for forgiveness."

"What if I don't care about forgiveness?" Kaye's eyes became mere slits. "And don't you have to mean it first?"

"Of course. I'll pick it up for you, Lorene." Claire retrieved the ball and handed it over.

Lorene's braces glimmered within her open-mouth smile. "Thank you."

Kaye blinked and stood near Wendy.

She decided their plan just might work. If she correctly read the more humbled look on Kaye Tyner's face.

~∧~∧~

A knock came loud on the basement door, and Lizbeth ran to open it. Miss Rose entered with a huge smile on her face. She waved. "Hi, ladies. I've been invited to help you make pizza for your supper." Her index finger poked her glasses higher on her nose. "Won't that be fun?"

Lizbeth and Claire nodded. The other BG's jaws drooped as they were not aware of the rest of the plan Claire had shared with only Lizbeth. Kaye stood stone still. Wendy fluttered her lashes as though confused.

"Ya little smarty," Belinda whispered, "nice thinkin'." Claire beamed.

Miss Rose chatted with one girl and then another as Lizbeth placed on the counter all they would need for making pizza. When it was time, Miss Rose gave a cooking lesson on how to make pizza dough. Belinda volunteered to roll out the dough while everyone else chopped meats and vegetables for the toppings.

As this took place, the Lavender Girls stood back a bit as though leery of the teacher's presence.

After the meal and clean up, Lizbeth brought out checkers, chess, and a deck of cards. She set the games on the table. Wendy and Lorene played checkers on the floor. Kaye and Claire sat on the bed with the deck of cards. Lizbeth and Belinda played chess at the table.

Miss Rose had brought her knitting and settled into the only overstuffed chair to work on her project. From time to time, Claire noticed Miss Rose would glance around and nod, always with a slight smile. She wasn't at all sure they would need Miss Rose to intervene, but if they did she was there to guide them.

At first, she had to talk Kaye into playing cards. She agreed only if she could shuffle them and go first. The two girls sat cross legged from each other.

She smoothed her skirt. "Do you know how to play memory?"

"Sure. It's easy." Kaye placed each card face side down between them. "I'll spread them out."

The game went well, until Kaye took another turn on Claire's time.

"I'm next."

"No. You're not. Now you're a cheater."

She raised her voice. "You believe I would cheat?"

"Since that's what you're doing. Yes."

The other girls' chatter silenced. The other BGs stood next to where she and Kaye sat. Claire glanced at Miss Rose as she lay aside her knitting.

Belinda clasped her hands together. "Sometimes when I'm playing cards with my grandma, I've cheated. But I've never known Claire to cheat."

Kaye clamped her mouth shut.

Belinda waited. No one said a word. Wendy rose from her spot on the floor. "Kaye, did she really cheat?"

Kaye's face wrinkled. "Maybe I'm mistaken."

The BGs stared at Wendy. Claire figured none of them expected this from Wendy Lavender.

Kaye's shoulders sagged. "I guess I should say I'm sorry."

Claire gazed at Miss Rose and she nodded. "All's forgiven, Kaye." She touched the top of Kaye's head and her head jerked. "Why are you all being so nice?"

Startled at the question, and because she was the one accused, Claire answered that. "We want your friendship." She touched Kaye arm. "I mean this in the kindest way." She looked around. "Isn't it true we want to befriend Kaye?"

Everyone nodded—even Wendy.

The bully shot from the bed like one of those geysers Claire learned about in science class. "I've had enough." She stumbled and squeezed between the girls. "You're all a bunch of sappy do-gooders." She stomped across the room and slammed the bathroom door behind her.

Belinda tapped her foot. "That didn't go too swell."

"We need to give her some space." Wendy's brows rose under her curly bangs. "She's not used to so much kindness."

Lizbeth gasped. "Why not?"

"It's her mom. To put it nicely, she's controlling. And I've never heard her give Kaye one compliment. I've known Kaye and her family my whole life, so I'm not exaggerating." Her shoulders slumped. "Kaye has it rough."

"Gee."

"We sure didn't know."

"Wish we woulda' known sooner."

Lord, help us, help her.

Wendy shrugged. "She'll give me the silent treatment for days if she finds out I've told you."

Claire sat back down on the bed. "We won't say anything."

Kaye did not appear from the bathroom for a long while, and in that time, Miss Rose spoke to the little group in hushed tones about walking in one another shoes to understand the hurt someone has gone through. A few of the girls got teary-eyed. Some of them bowed their heads. Claire understood how harsh life could be.

When Kaye returned, the whites of her eyes were bloodshot. Her face puffy. She changed into her pajamas and crawled into the bed by the corner wall.

The girls played more games at the table, ate some cookies and chips and soon began to yawn.

Everyone had dressed in their pajamas while Miss Rose continued to knit in the overstuffed chair.

Wendy sat on the bed Belinda and Claire had taken. "Belinda?" She inhaled deeply. "I need to apologize."

Belinda sat up against the headboard. "Really?"

"I'm sorry I called you those awful names back in Gallagher Springs. Especially when I called you scar face." She lowered her lashes.

Everyone jumped when Kaye yelled, "What are you doing, Wendy? Now they have you confessing." The snarl on Kaye's face would scare a grown man.

Wendy stared at her from across the room. "I had no right to call Belinda names."

Kaye bounded from her bed. She got within inches of her face. "Why are you caving?"

"Kaye." She placed a hand on each of her shoulders. "You know what our dads do at their jobs, right?"

"Of course."

"Think of this. Our dads are blasting through a mountain to make a way for progress. For faster travel from one city to another. Just like that example, you and I have an opportunity to blast through the walls we've built around ourselves. To share our problems and secrets with these girls who want our friendship." She waved a hand at the others. "Some of them have opened up to us. Let's share with them our problems." Wendy tugged at the leg of Kaye's pajama bottom. "You as well are imperfect."

She jerked from Wendy so hard, she stumbled backwards. "Don't you dare." She growled the words. "You can tell your secrets, but leave me alone." Kaye took a backward step from the others. "You are all freaks."

The tallest girl there blocked her path. "What is it ya feel ya have to hide, Miss Kaye?"

"It's nothing as bad as your face, Cruz."

The BGs gasped. All of them faced Miss Rose.

Once again, Miss Rose lay aside her knitting. "What if I tell you a secret about myself, Kaye?" She stood from her chair. "No one's going to laugh at you. No one is going to cringe in horror. It may surprise us, and that's all." She took off her glasses and squinted. "Like no one here is horrified that without my glasses, your face is a total blur." She touched near her eye. "They are beady. Not shaped like normal eyes.

Claire had never noticed before.

Miss Rose continued. "When I was in elementary school, children called me squint eyes and four eyes. It hurt to hear those words, but once the kids grew older and were in junior high, no one said a word about my need for glasses. Or the extra small shape of my eyes."

Wendy angled her head. "Go ahead, Kaye. These girls have compassion. I call them friends."

She puckered her mouth into a knot.

"Okay, I'll go next." Wendy glanced at every girl. "My mother ran away from home last year. My parents are divorcing. My dad keeps me with him because he's afraid Mom will steal me, and he'll never see me again."

Kaye covered her ears. "Don't tell your darkest secret." She slumped onto the bed behind her. "I promised Mother. I would never, ever let anyone see them. She said it was too grotesque. That no one would want to be my friend if they knew." Kaye bowed her face into her hands. "Mother says I'm ugly."

Wendy knelt on one knee before Kaye. "It's not true." Kaye laid her face on her lap and cried and rocked. Wendy touched her head. "Will you ever see that your mother is a bully?"

"She's not. She's not." She fell forward on her knees into Wendy's open arms.

The other girls became a huddle around the Lavender Girls. There were *shhh's*, *it's okays*, and *go ahead and let it out*. Lizbeth was sobbing.

Claire whispered into Kaye's ear, "You have to trust someone, sometime. We hope you will begin with us." Her heart stung for her misery.

Lizbeth disappeared and came back with tissues for Kaye. She blew her nose. While her sobs became sniffles, Kaye lifted her one pajama pant. "See, I'm like Frankenstein's monster." Her entire leg including her knee was stained with purple-colored skin.

Miss Rose knelt next to Kaye. "This is why you wear colored tights? Why you wouldn't wear the gym-issued suit for PE?" Miss Rose patted Kaye's hand. "From now on, honey, wear the gym suit with your colored tights underneath."

Kaye hiccupped.

"That ain't nothin' but a birthmark. Trade ya any day, Kaye Tyner. I wish I had a grape leg and not my scars. And I've got ya beat as the monster."

"No, you don't."

"Yeah, I do."

"You don't."

"I do."

First one girl giggled. Then another. Until, everyone was bent over in laughter.

Claire took a backward step from the ruckus. Was this possible? Had they really, finally made friends with Wendy Lavender? And now Kaye Tyner?

Deep within her, she believed it was true. What she couldn't do back in Gallagher Springs with the Lavender Girls happened here in Lizbeth's basement. A new idea hit like a roar of thunder.

"Hey." Claire clapped to get their attention. "I say we six become the Bold Believers Club." Her hands swung in melodramatic flare. "You know as in we believe in each other and the Lord. Do we want to take a vote?"

All the girls said, "No." Except Kaye. She nodded.

"Really?"

Everyone talked at once.

What Claire understood was they didn't need to vote. They agreed for everyone being friends in the Bold Believers Club.

Claire grinned so broadly she just knew it would be plastered on her face for the entire school year.

The End

Season of the Fawns

Available Summer 2021

1

I SHALL NOT WANT

VALE

Vale shifted her Jeep, a CJ7, into first gear and stopped for a rusty, bullet-ridden stop sign. She checked the watch fastened on her freckled wrist. "I hope he didn't have a bad night." After his climbing accident two months ago on Watch Tower Mountain, her cousin Caleb suffered with monster headaches caused from his head injury.

She rolled into Caleb's weed-invested driveway and halted next to his pickup. The swinging bridge their grandfather, "Papa", had built long ago stood as a guard, yet welcoming. She grabbed a woven basket off the passenger seat filled with Caleb's favorite foods. Her western boots hit the ground with a thud. Vale breathed deeply the smells of the last days of autumn, dried leaves and grasses beneath a blue sky. A breeze swished her russet brown hair across her cheeks.

She threw the Jeep keys in the air. The sun reflected off the metal as they soared over the roll bar and plopped on the driver's seat. Perfect toss.

As Vale readjusted her grip on the basket, she couldn't wait to talk with Caleb about next week. They would celebrate their twentieth birthdays during their yearly hunting trip.

Vale's boot twisted sideways on pine cones, and she whirled her arm to gain her balance. "When is he ever going to rake Papa's walkway?" Swinging her free arm in a hurried pace, she reached the wooden bridge. She steadied herself with one hand on the taut, rusty logging cable Papa used to attach the railing. With the sway of the bridge, her memories flowed. She was a little girl again at her grandparents' cottage. As Vale's boot met with hard ground, the past swaddled her like a thick quilt.

Now that Nana and Papa had passed away and gone to the Great Beyond, the cottage was Caleb's.

She stomped up the porch steps and stood before the rough-hewed wood door. The knob wouldn't budge. "Hey, Caleb, open up." She peeked through the door's crisscross window panes. Clothes were scattered across the floor, sofa, and even over Jimmy Bird's now vacant cage. Even birds don't live forever.

She tapped on the glass with her short fingernails. "Hey, cuz, I made your favorite Pastrami on a French roll." She raised her voice. "With extra mustard and Ma's pickled cucs."

Vale set their lunch on the redwood floorboards. She walked over the bridge and retrieved her keys. Back at the door, she stuck in the key and twisted. As she pushed the door groaned. The air inside smelled musty and wise—like her grandparents. Since they were gone, the ache in Vale's heart stretched. Like a giant hole in the earth left by the exposed roots of an old growth tree.

She propped the piggy door stopper against the kick plate, one of dozens of pigs from Grandma Nana's collections. Vale slid the basket on in with the side of her western boot and frowned. "Gross. Caleb." She smelled more than wisdom as she walked through the middle of the living area. When did Caleb become such a slob?

Vale's once tidy cousin now lived in clutter, cobwebs, and leftover rotting food. The word slob was too harsh of a word for someone who had been meticulous. She paved a trail with her boots, forcing clothes and a few to-go containers through the cottage.

The clicking of dog toenails sounded from the kitchen. Vale watched the kitchen doorway, and Kippy rounded the corner from the kitchen. Reaching down to pet Caleb's tri-Aussie, Kippy bee-lined past her and ran out the door. "Well, a fine howdy to you too." She shook her head and chuckled at the dog. She always had something to do and in a hurry.

She moved to a closed door. "Caleb?" Vale pressed her ear near the door jamb. "Are you ready in there? Did you remember our picnic?" Twisting the glass knob, she shoved against the warped door and into Grandma's old sewing room. Closed shutters over the bay window let in slants of light. The large sofa Caleb used as a bed filled the room, bare of sheets and blankets. Vale's brows waggled in a worry-wart dance. She stepped over his sawdust-covered jeans and opened an adjoining door to their grandparents' bedroom.

Caleb—Vale rushed to a mattress on the floor. His light brown head of hair and shoulders had slumped off the bed. She pressed fingers into his neck to feel for a pulse. Finding a heart rhythm, she sighed with relief. After Vale lugged him onto his pillow, she nudged his shoulder. "Caleb, wake up." She touched his cool cheek and with the other hand fished her cell phone from the pocket of her western riding skirt. She punched buttons as she trembled.

"911. What is your emergency?"

"My cousin needs an ambulance. 2020 Rifle Creek Road, fifteen minutes past Forest Glen Retirement Center in Forest Glen."

Twenty minutes later, the operator still had Vale on the phone as she instructed her to keep a check on Caleb's pulse. As Vale gave another pulse report to the operator, she broke off in mid-sentence with the sound of sirens. "They're here," and Vale disconnected the call with the 911 operator. The sobs she had been controlling now boiled over like cowboy coffee on a blazing campfire. The medical team moved in with one swoop, and Vale leaned against the wall a few feet away. They assessed Caleb's condition. After what seemed like an eternity, with questions thrown at her she couldn't answer, the team carried her cousin on a gurney to the ambulance.

In her Jeep, Vale followed the ambulance to the hospital in Griffins Pass. Once they drove through Forest Glen and onto the freeway, she gained control of her shakes. She pressed the name on her cell and waited only seconds. "Hello."

"Ma!" Vale's voice broke. She veered off toward the shoulder but swerved. Vale was back into her lane.

Rodell Cutter, Vale's ma, replied. "What's going on, baby?"

"I'm okay, but it's Caleb." She nodded with her ear to the phone at her mother's question. "Yes, he's on the way to the hospital. I found him unconscious."

Ma's words were clipped and stern. "What happened?"

Tears blurred her vision, and she blinked. "I'm not sure, but the ambulance guy grabbed Caleb's bottle of pills from the top of Nana's old dresser."

"Oh, dear Lord." Ma spoke in a near whisper. "I hope he didn't do this on purpose."

Vale yelled, "Don't say that just because of Papa."

"I'm sorry. Maybe it's something else." Ma sighed. "I'll meet you at the hospital."

"Okay, Ma." Vale clicked off her phone and tossed it to the passenger seat.

Curvy roads down one of the mountain passes became a hair-pin and required her full attention. The last time she begged God for help was when Caleb fell on the mountain. "Dear, Lord, please keep him alive." She trusted God heard her words.

But, she also understood His will may not be her will.

Vale's foot was like lead on the gas pedal as she came upon a straight stretch of road. Ahead of her, the ambulance continued to flash its lights. Caleb seemed so far and away. *Could it be forever?*

It took the fourth mountain pass, and entering the valley to calm her nerves. The landscape spread before her with vivid green firs accented with the red bark of the bold madrones. Dotted within were some trees with a few fall-colored leaves left on almost bare branches.

After thirty miles of driving, she took the exit leading to Griffins Pass. Six traffic lights stood between her and the hospital. By now, Ma would be waiting for her in the emergency room.

She frowned as she remembered Ma's comment—the thought ripped like a buck knife. *Was Papa's death really not an accident?* He'd been on various medications for different ailments, including narcolepsy. Almost a year ago, Papa stopped his medications all at once the day before Thanksgiving. He died from a Grand Mal Seizure.

Vale geared down, slowing to enter the ER parking lot. She pulled the CJ7 into a narrow space, cut the engine, and leaped from the seat. Slipping her keys in her corduroy pocket, she patted the other where her wallet was safely nestled. At the automatic doors, she stalled to wait for them to open. Running inside, she stopped as if she'd hit a wall. *Where's Ma?* She held her hands near her chin as if in prayer and searched the crowded lobby.

There. Ma hunched over a water fountain, her bowed legs bent, and splashed water on her flushed cheeks. *She's crying?* Very few times had Vale seen Ma gush with emotion—happy or sad.

Wiping her hands on the back pockets of her boot-cut jeans, Vale's ma swiveled. The two women met in the middle of the room where Vale launched into her ma's arms. She sniffed. "How soon until we hear?"

"I checked in with the receptionist." Ma brushed Vale's wild, brown curls from her face. "Honey, they have to stabilize him."

With Ma a half a foot taller, Vale craned her neck. "Stabilize?"

"Yes. I'm sure Caleb's in bad shape, *if* he indeed took more than he should have of his medication."

Clenching her fingers, Vale made a squeal noise at the back of her throat.

Ma grabbed Vale's fist and pulled her toward the French Brothers coffee hut. "I'll get us something to drink."

Vale relaxed her hand within her ma's, blinking, blinking against the blur of moisture in her eyes.

Hot drinks in hand, they found a quiet table. Vale's lashes fluttered in concentration between sips of mocha. And she knew she had to talk about what happened. From before. "Caleb hasn't been doing well ever since he fell on Watch Tower Mountain."

Ma shook her head. "No, he hasn't."

"I pray our yearly birthday hunting trip will change things for him." Vale swallowed another mouthful of the rich liquid. "You know, perk him up."

Ma set down her cup. "You may have to cancel your trip."

"It's not for a whole week." Vale leaned forward with a jerk, sloshing mocha over the rim of the thick paper cup. "I'll nurse Caleb back to health before then. You just watch."

"Vale." Ma sighed long and slow. "Don't start."

"But, Ma." She pursed her lips. "He can't miss our yearly hunt. This would be like giving in to his troubles, and Caleb's not a quitter." A knot formed in her throat, and she swallowed it along with another gulp of her drink.

"I hope you're right about Caleb." She squeezed her daughter's arm. "People can be pushed to their limits, Lord only knows."

There it is again. She means Papa.

The receptionist called from behind her counter, "Mrs. Cutter?"

Vale shot forward from her chair. "Is Caleb ready?"

Ma hurried around the table, circled an arm around Vale's shoulders, and together they slowed their walking to a normal pace toward the lady.

The receptionist smiled. "I'll show you to Mr. Cutter's cubicle." She pointed. "Meet me at the double doors to your right."

Ma reached for Vale's hand, and they both hung on.

^~^~^

A nurse stood outside the closed curtain.

Vale touched her chest. "I'm Caleb's cousin, Vale, and this is my mother, Rodell."

"I'm Siri." The nurse looked from one to the other. "You're the closest of kin?"

Vale nodded. "My parents adopted him, because his folks died when he was ten years old. So he and I are also siblings."

The nurse raised her brows. "Caleb had a close call with his medication."

Ma's lips trembled from her own question. "Was it intentional?"

Vale glared at her ma.

"The little amount we pumped from his stomach?" Siri let go a long breath. "It's hard to tell, except his dose direction's say to take only one."

"So it's possible it was an accident?" Vale winced, hoping, hoping.

Siri rested the clipboard with Caleb's information against her chest. "Taking even one more than the prescribed amount is considered an overdose."

Clasping her hands together, Ma twisted her fingers. It was as though ice water raced along Vale's spine. "I need to see him."

"Remember, he's sore and exhausted." Siri touched Vale's arm. "He probably won't feel like talking."

Vale moved closer to the curtain. "Thank you, ma'am." She locked eyes with Ma. "May I go in first?" Ma nodded, and Vale separated the drape with a swish along the metal rod. She breathed in and out and forced a pleasant expression. For Caleb.

 Jean Ann Williams lives on the Coast of Oregon with her husband Jim. She began her writing career in 1994 by reading a stack of books on the craft of writing. Since then, Jean Ann has published over 300 articles and short stories on the topics of Christianity, health, travel, friendship, relationships, family life, Sunday school take-home papers, and the loss of a child by suicide. In her free time, Jean Ann enjoys Tunisian Crocheting, reading inspirational books, gardening, and playing Scrabble with her grandchildren. Sometimes they let Nana win.

To learn more about Jean Ann Williams, visit her on Facebook Author Page: https://bit.ly/3iYLJAj
Twitter: https://twitter.com/JeanAnnWilliams

Just Claire

One mother damaged. One family tested. One daughter determined to find her place.

ClaireLee's life changes when she must take charge of her siblings because her mother becomes depressed after a difficult childbirth. Frightened by the way Mama sleeps too much and her crying spells during waking hours, ClaireLee just knows she'll catch her illness like a cold or flu that hangs on through winter. ClaireLee finds comfort in the lies she tells herself and others in order to hide the truth about her erratic mother. Deciding she needs to re-invent herself, she sets out to impress a group of popular girls.

With her deception, ClaireLee weaves her way into the Lavender Girls Club, the most sophisticated girls in school. Though, her best friend Belinda will not be caught with the likes of such shallow puddles, ClaireLee ignores Belinda's warnings the Lavenders cannot be trusted. ClaireLee drifts farther from honesty, her friend, and a broken mother's love, until one very public night at the yearly school awards ceremony. The spotlight is on her, and she finds her courage and faces the truth and then ClaireLee saves her mother's life.

Amazon: https://amzn.to/3nKnzwZ

Just Claire Book Trailer:
https://youtu.be/s8x5lJKZFHU
Goodreads *Just Claire*:
https://www.goodreads.com/book/show/28482298-just-claire

Road Trip of Delusion

Fifteen-year-old Kari Rose discovers how much trouble she and her two sisters can get into when they stay at their ancient granny's for spring break. Granny gets a wild-haired notion at three in the morning, and she's leaving with or without them. Kari makes the decision to take her sisters and ride with Granny in her old Cadillac on a five-hundred-mile-long trip north to visit family. Miles down the road, this harmless act finds Granny no longer able to drive, and Kari must take the wheel. Soon after, the four travelers are caught in a freeway-closing-down snowstorm which brings everyone and everything to a standstill.

A second blizzard with catastrophic impact is about to descend upon them, and Kari must determine the best way to find shelter and beat the storm. Will Kari trust her gut instincts and rely upon a complete stranger to lead them to safety? **Amazon:** https://amzn.to/2lvyjz6

God's Mercies after Suicide

What if your child shot himself while you were in the next room? What if you held him as his heart beat for the last time? What if Satan whispered in your ear, "Now where is your God?" Find out how Jean Ann Williams reached out with her spirit and mind to the one true Father. Discover how the Lord God answered her, and walked alongside her in the most difficult grieving journey of her life.

Amazon: https://goo.gl/wju4dm
God's Mercies after Suicide **Book Trailer:**
https://youtu.be/yvNDlNHEyok
http://Joshua-mom.blogspot.com/

A Pocket Full of Memories

Mother's Day for Dotty Monteiro begins with four cards and ends with an unexpected turn of events. As she and her husband Pete anticipate phone calls from their five children, she quietly prays for visits and a chance to laugh together as a family and hug her children. But where is Lolly, the daughter who felt displaced when the youngest was born? She hasn't been home for three years. Not a call or a card in so long. What Dotty would give to see her daughter again!

Dotty has a long-time faith in Christ and knows God always hears her prayers. But she also knows sometimes they are met with silence. How will her Mother's Day unfold this year? Will it be a repeat of years past? When will she experience the Mother's Day of her heart's desire?

Jean Ann Williams introduced the young Monteiro children in her previous book, *Just Claire*. Now leap into their future as adults with their own families.

Amazon: https://amzn.to/33ZPmBL
Amazon Author Page: https://amzn.to/3lOlZbk
Twitter: https://twitter.com/JeanAnnWilliams
Facebook Author Page: https://bit.ly/31lI9iD
Pinterest: https://www.pinterest.com/jeanann_w/
Instagram: https://www.instagram.com/jeanann_w/
Goodreads Author Page: https://bit.ly/3jO3lvk

www.ingramcontent.com/pod-product-compliance
Lightning Source LLC
Chambersburg PA
CBHW021219250626
47155CB00008B/2879